MW00932822

The characters and events portrayed in this book are fictitious. Any similarity to real persons, living or dead, is coincidental and not intended by the author. Any reference to real locations is only for atmospheric effect, and in no way truly represents those locations.

Published by Higher Bank Books

CONTAGION RISING

A Post Apocalyptic Zombie Thriller

THE INFECTED CHRONICLES
BOOK 2

RYAN CASEY

GET A POST APOCALYPTIC NOVEL FOR FREE

To instantly receive an exclusive post apocalyptic novel totally free, sign up for Ryan Casey's author newsletter at: ryancasey books.com/fanclub

DIMITRI

"Are you feeling alright, pal?"

Dimitri's arms tingled. *Pal.* He hated that word. One of his least favourite English words. These Brits threw it about way too readily. Dimitri didn't have many friends back home. But even the closest ones, he'd never dream of calling "Pal."

He turned around.

Jimmy stared at him. His eyes bulged wide. Sweat trickled down his forehead and his hairy chest. The smell of sweat radiated from his body, filling Dimitri's nostrils, making him want to puke. The sun beamed down from above, scorching, intense. Dimitri usually liked the sun. He never got the sun back home much. And sun wasn't something that was on the list of expectations when he came to Britain three months ago.

But right now... right now, he'd do anything for a cool, dark room.

"You look a bit pale," Jimmy said. "A bit purple round the eyes. Heavy night?"

Dimitri turned away. He shovelled some cement on the bricks in front of him with his shaking hand, and then planted another brick on top of it. Beneath him, some thug in a high vis and no top on pissed in the corner of this work-in-progress new build. One of his mates laughed at him. Joined him. Animals. Absolute animals. And it was always the Brits who treated their own constructions with no respect, while migrant workers like him worked their arses off in pursuit of perfection.

No wonder this pointless island was going to shit.

"Thugs, ain't they?"

Dimitri closed his burning eyes. Why wouldn't this bastard just shut up? He wanted to get on with his job. He wasn't here to make friends. Or "pals". He was here to work, to earn his cash, and then to go home and call Nadia. The only thing he looked forward to in life these days. Getting a good day's work done. Getting home, opening FaceTime, and speaking to Nadia all evening. Some blokes went to the pub. Others watched shitty television shows, and played FIFA with their mates. Not Dimitri. As long as he had Nadia, Dimitri had no use for any of that shit.

"You know, I know it ain't easy. Coming here from abroad. Fitting in, and all that."

Jesus, was this guy *still* talking? Didn't he get the message? Dimitri wasn't interested.

Best to just keep on laying bricks. Keep on building this house. Keep on pretending like Jimmy wasn't speaking at all.

"Your girl. You must miss her."

A fire ignited in Dimitri's chest. He turned around. Jimmy looked over at him, shirt off, holding a brick.

"What did you say?" Dimitri asked.

Jimmy smiled. "Thought that might get your attention. I see you sneakin' off at lunch for a phone call."

Dimitri's face turned hot. Bastard. Stalking bastard. Nadia was none of his business. His relationship with Nadia was no business of *anyone* here.

He grabbed another brick. His hand shook. Shit, his head was aching like mad, and he couldn't stop yawning. Felt like he was living in slow motion like his brain was sitting in a haze of fog.

"I'm not tryin' to pry or anythin'. I'm just... I'm just sayin'. If ever you wanna grab a brew. Or a beer. Or anything. I'm here. That's all."

Dimitri looked back at Jimmy. Cracking on with his work now, laying more bricks as the pair of them crouched there on the scaffolding. Hell, he wanted to tell this nosy bastard to piss off. But at the same time... a knot tightened in his chest. 'Cause Jimmy was only trying to help. He didn't seem a thug, or a waster. Not like the others.

"Thank you," Dimitri said.

Jimmy looked at him. Smiled. "My pleasure. Now go get some water or summat. You look like you're about to die right there. And I don't wanna be peeling your body off the tarmac below any time soon." He chuckled, laughing at his own sick joke.

Truth be told, Dimitri hadn't felt right ever since his caving trip at the weekend. Nadia moaned that he should do something he enjoyed—something that didn't involve her, or work. And sure, he felt kind of pathetic admitting there was nothing he really wanted to do that didn't involve her. But it was true. It really was true. She was the only person he wanted to do anything with.

But Nadia wasn't moving over here any time soon. He didn't want to stay here too long, either. Make a good bit of cash, then move back to Poland, find some cheap property in the countryside, and live off-grid, growing their own produce, looking after their own animals, selling eggs to villagers, all that stuff.

A lump swelled in his throat when he thought of Nadia. That future with her. A future he was desperate to secure, as soon as he possibly could.

But Nadia was right. He couldn't be over-reliant on her for his happiness. He needed to have fun—even if it was just under the pretence of "having fun" just to get her off his case. So he'd gone caving. Had a look for local caves. Nothing too amateur; he'd been into caving for years. One of his favourite ways of truly switching off from the outside world. The darkness. The sound of dripping water. The smell of freshness, a reminder of the very earth beneath our feet. That was truly Dimitri's happy place.

It was on his way out that he felt the sharp pain on his left forearm. He looked down with his head torch, saw a pair of tooth-marks there, and blood trickling out. A bat? Probably. Which worried him a bit, because bats could be rabid, couldn't they?

He got out of the cave and the pain eased. He didn't think about it again. Didn't tell Nadia about it. She'd only tease him and tell him he was going to turn into Batman, which would annoy him because Batman wasn't like Spiderman—he didn't get bit by a bat and turn into a bloody bat man.

But now...

Dizziness.

Dry mouth.

Shaking. And crippling stomach pains.

What if it was to do with the bite?

He rolled up his sleeve. The skin around the wound glowed an angry red. Pus trickled out of the scabbed tooth marks. And... and was that a *smell* radiating from it? A nasty smell, like... an earthiness? Almost like he was back down in those caves, but the dream had turned into a nightmare, and—

"Shit, pal."

That voice. That *frigging* voice.

Jimmy stared at Dimitri's arm with wide eyes.

"You get bit by a snake or summat?"

"It's nothing," Dimitri said, rolling down his sleeve, and reaching for another brick.

"It don't look like nothin' to me. You wanna go get that checked out."

Dimitri lifted the brick. His cheeks burned even hotter. "I'm fine."

"I'm just sayin'—"

"I'm *fine*, okay?"

Jimmy's eyes widened. He held up his hands. "Hey. I'm just trying to help, pal. Just trying to help."

Shit. Dimitri couldn't go flipping like that. He'd end up getting himself fired. And besides. In his irritating way, this Jimmy prick was only trying to help, wasn't he?

Dimitri took a long, deep breath of the warm summer air. "I'm sorry," he said.

Jimmy waved a hand at him.

"I will... I will go get it checked. I will go get water. You want drink?"

Jimmy glanced up at him. Narrowed his eyes. Like he was weighing up whether to trust Dimitri or not. "Sure," he said. "I'll have a coffee. But don't put too much milk in. Or it'll..."

A sudden blast of earthiness filled Dimitri's nostrils.

Screaming.

Screaming in his skull.

White noise.

No. Not white noise. Nadia. Nadia's screaming.

And then... and then he heard a voice. A voice, cutting through the silence. Jimmy's voice.

"He just—he just collapsed!" Jimmy screamed. "Ambulance is on its way. You're gonna be okay, pal. You're gonna be okay..."

But Dimitri didn't feel okay.

Dimitri's skin burned.

Burned with something like... something like rage.

Pure, unfiltered rage.

And in his mind's eye, he saw all kinds of horrid scenarios in front of him.

He saw Jimmy.

He saw him raping Nadia.

He saw her screaming with pleasure or pain and then blood splattering everywhere and the word PAL written across the walls in her blood and—

"You're gonna be okay," Jimmy said, a hand on Dimitri's shoulder. "You're gonna be…"

And then Jimmy was holding Nadia's head, holding her severed head and moving his tongue towards her gaping jaw and…

No.

No he couldn't let that happen.

He had to make him pay.

He had to make him—

BITE.

He launched himself at Jimmy and he wrapped his teeth around his throat and he bit down and he tasted warm metallic water and he kept biting as Jimmy kicked and screamed and blood splattered everywhere and he hit him again and again with that brick, again and again as people ran over, as people tried to drag him away, as people tried to stop him…

And all the time, as they dragged him away, as they restrained him, all he wanted was to hurt them.

All he wanted was to hurt these bastards.

All he wanted was to mess these pricks up.

All he wanted was to…

Bite.

The smell of the earthiness of the cave consumed him, as in his mind's eye, he saw that bat, flying away, blood trickling from its sharp little teeth…

DAVID

* * *

David looked into Keira's eyes and even though he was in the middle of a goddamned nightmare, he felt like he was dreaming.

Screaming echoed around the front of the hospital. Thick smoke filled his lungs, making him choke. He couldn't breathe properly. Felt like someone was slicing the insides of his lungs with little knives. A metallic tang clung to his lips. Blood. His arms were burning, too. Tingling, burning, really sore. A woman raced past, covered in blood. She tumbled over. Looked over her shoulder with wide eyes at some unseen, oncoming threat. And then she stumbled back to her feet. Started running again. Constant reminders of the danger they were in, all around.

But David didn't care.

Harsh as it might sound, he really didn't care.

Because Keira was here.

Keira looked back at him with wide brown eyes. Brown eyes that hadn't changed since she was a little baby. Those eyes were the feature people always commented on: strangers in the super-

market, doctors in the surgery. And those eyes had witnessed so
many horrors. Those eyes had witnessed so much pain. Even
when she was a baby, Keira had a fight on her hands. She
contracted a rare blood vessel disorder when she was very young.
Kawasaki syndrome. And while usually, Kawasaki syndrome was
manageable, Keira's case took a sinister turn, leaving her hospi-
talised for weeks.

David would never forget lying by her side. Holding her little
hand. Stroking her scorching forehead. "It's going to be okay, little
girl. I promise you everything's going to be okay."

A pain swelled in the middle of his chest.

The years since.

Everything that happened since.

But she was here now.

She was here, and in the midst of chaos, everything was going
to be okay. He was going to put everything right.

"It's so good to see y…"

Keira turned away. Looked at this Asian fella beside her, the
one who'd told David she'd gone into the children's ward. "You
should be with your wife. With your children."

The man nodded. He half-smiled at her. "And you should
remember my words."

He glanced over at David. Then back at Keira again.

"The children," he said, looking around at the small group of
kids gathered around. "I will care for as many of them as I can."

"Nitesh, you shouldn't have to—"

"I have a big home and a very playful pair of daughters. Right
now, while this… while this blows over, they need me. Trust me.
It's what I want."

Keira nodded. Lowered her head.

"Good luck," Keira said.

The man—Nitesh—looked at David again. Forced a smile,
amidst the panic, amidst the chaos. "And you too."

He turned away. Then stopped. Looked back at Keira. "And thank you."

"For what?"

He smiled. "For lifting me up. In my lowest moment. And for being rather good lift company."

She smiled back at him. Looked like tears were forming in her eyes.

And then this man turned away and he ran away, with the children from the ward, holding them close.

Keira watched him leave. And—and David could barely even speak. His daughter. His girl. She was here. She was right here.

But... the screaming.

The sirens.

The scorching heat, radiating from behind.

They were still in danger here. Big danger.

He looked down at Rufus, who wagged his tail upon eye contact. Then at Keira.

"I'm sure—I'm sure your friend will be okay," David said. He didn't know what to say. What the hell was he supposed to say? He hadn't seen his daughter in years. And now she was here, right in front of him... it wasn't the reunion he imagined.

"We need—we need to get away from here," David said. "We need to get to safety."

Home flashed into mind. Mrs Kirkham. Her nurse. The blood. All that blood. A bitter taste filled David's mouth. Was home safe? And if it wasn't... where was?

"Come on," David said. "We... we need to get away from here. It's not safe here."

"There's somewhere I need to go," Keira said.

She wasn't looking into David's eyes anymore. She was staring off into the distance, wide-eyed.

"Keira—"

"A friend. I made... I made a promise to a friend."

"And that's all fair and good. But—but it's not safe here."

Keira started walking. She... she'd barely even *acknowledged* him, after dragging him out of the hospital. It was like water had been thrown on the moment of connection they'd had already; like the cold water of reality had put out the flame of reconnection in an instant. And now she was walking away somewhere. Not even looking at David.

David walked after her. "Keira. You—you can't just walk away."

Keira didn't stop. "There's someone I need to find."

"Right now you—you need to come back to mine, love. It's safe there. It's... it's quiet there. Not many people about. You need to come to mine with me and—and wait this out."

Keira stopped. She turned around to face David. A frown crept across her face. "I'm sorry, but *I* need to 'come back to yours'?"

David's face turned hot. No. Not now. He—he could see from the look on Keira's face that she wasn't happy. The way she tried to shut him down. And the way she tried to push him away. He'd seen it. He'd seen it so many times before. "I'm just trying to be realistic."

"Well I'm sorry, but the last time I checked, I was an adult woman. Capable of making my own decisions."

"And that's all fair and well," David said. "But right now, in case you haven't noticed, something's going down. Something big."

Keira's eyes widened, bloodshot. "Oh, I've noticed, alright. I sure noticed my friend being torn to shreds. I noticed a dozen of these infected bastards almost kill me. And I noticed an entire children's ward almost die because of them. Yeah. I noticed."

"I didn't mean it like that."

Keira shook her head, closed her eyes. "Look. I'm... I'm glad you're okay. I'm glad you're alive. But..." And then she looked up into his eyes. "But there's something I need to do. There's someone I need to find. And that's my decision."

Keira's words hit David like bullets to the chest. He'd... he'd found her. He'd come all this way to find her. And she was... she was turning him away? This wasn't the reunion he dreamed of. This was the reunion of nightmares.

But wasn't this how it was always ever going to go, anyway?

"I just... I just care," David said. "I'm your dad, Keira. And I... I care."

"Well you've chosen a funny time to start caring," Keira said.

Those words. David *felt* them viscerally. Like a punch to the gut.

Keira looked into his eyes again. Her eyes flickered. Twitched. Water built inside them. Like when she was sad. Like when she was a kid, and she just wanted a hug, or a bedtime story.

But she wasn't a kid anymore. And she didn't want a hug, or a bedtime story.

She wanted... something else.

She opened her mouth to say something else.

And then, to the left, David heard it.

A scream.

No. No, more than one scream.

Loads of screams.

David turned around.

People. A crowd of people, racing towards him. A dark-haired woman holding a child. A man, pushing a pram. And an old woman holding on to an old man, trying to help her get away from whatever was coming.

Rufus growled.

"What's..." David muttered.

And then, out of nowhere, a woman lunged on top of the old man. Wrestled him to the ground. The woman, she looked barely out of her teens. She climbed up his body, and then she sunk her teeth into his throat. The man struggled. Scratched at the concrete with his skinny fingers. The old woman beside him howled, holding his arm, trying to cling on to him. Around him, the crowd screamed. But none of them stopped. All of them ran on past. And behind them... more of these people. More of these pursuers.

David's stomach turned. A shiver raced down his spine. He stood there, mouth drying up, Rufus growling by his side.

"They're here," he said.

And then the girl ripped the old woman's throat out, and looked right up into David's eyes, with that dead-eyed glare.

NISHA

* * *

Nisha held the man called Dwayne's hand and ran down the slope out of the car park.

Dwayne's warm hand tightened around hers. And she didn't know who this man was. She knew what Dad always told her about not trusting strangers. And she'd just found out why for herself. The man who made her get into his car. The man who turned the knife on her. The man she only just got away from, *because* of Dwayne.

Nisha's heart raced. She felt dizzy and she felt sick. Visions of Beth filled her mind. Behind that window. Scratching at it with her long fingernails. Biting at it with her teeth.

And then Ginger Harry, and Mrs Thompson, and everyone at the school.

All the blood.

All the guts.

All the...

The sickly feeling in her belly grew heavier. She tried to breathe, but she couldn't. She—she was choking. She was dying.

She had a snake around her throat and it was getting tighter, and tighter, and—and she couldn't run, she couldn't think, she couldn't move.

The dizzy feeling in her head got stronger.

The taste of blood on her lips.

And that snake around her neck, squeezing tighter, and tighter, and...

She stopped running. She stopped running and she planted her hands on her knees. Be strong. Be strong, Nisha. Be—be strong.

But she couldn't breathe. She couldn't breathe and she was going to die because she was so weak and so scared and...

The man. His hands on both of her shoulders. Turning her around. Staring into her eyes. His lips weren't moving. He was just... looking at her. He took a hand away from her shoulder. Pointed to her chest. Then moved it to his. His belly moved. Breathing in. That's—that's what he was pointing to. Breathing in.

She fought past the snake around her neck and her body and she breathed in. Deeply.

Then she breathed out.

Then in again.

Then out again.

Watching his breathing.

Following his breathing.

Then...

He smiled at her. Not a big smile. But... but just this little smile. A smile that told her she was going to be okay. That even though things were awful, everything was going to be okay, right now.

And then she saw movement behind him.

Her stomach turned to stone, all heavy. There—there was someone behind him. Someone... someone moving. Someone moving this way. Figures. Two—two of them. Walking between two cars. One of them—the man—moved like a robot. His hands twisted. He stretched out his fingers, which looked broken. And his eyes. His eyes were... dead.

The snake around her neck grew tighter again. But this time, she kept on breathing, remembering the rhythm Dwayne taught her.

She reached out to him. Slowly. Tapped on his shoulder. Then pointed to them, right behind him, the rest of her body still, the rest of her body like a stone on the ground.

His eyes widened. He turned around.

When he saw the two figures wandering around the entrance to the car park, blocking their way out, he froze for a second. Time stood still. Maybe if they were still, the infected wouldn't see them. Maybe she just had to stay still.

A memory flashed in her mind. Mrs Thompson. Holding her in that bathroom. Moving towards her. Trying to bite her. And then... and then just stopping. Stopping, and letting her go. A chance to get away.

Was that because she'd stayed still?

Dwayne turned back to her. He put a finger over his lips. And then he grabbed her hand, softly, and he led her back in the car park, back towards the cars.

Smashed bottles crunched under her feet. The graffiti on the brick walls of horrible things and of nasty words stared down at her. She didn't want to be in this place. She wanted to get away from this place.

But Dwayne pulled her back in here. Back towards the cars.

The bad people. Were they chasing her and Dwayne? Were they following them? She didn't even want to look over her shoulder to check.

And then Dwayne pulled her around the side of the car the bad man had kidnapped her in and crouched down with her.

He turned to her. Put a finger over his lips. And—and the tingling covered her body again, head to toe. Her heart beat so hard it felt like it was going to explode in her chest. Could hearts explode? She might be about to find out.

She looked up. Into the mirror at the side of the car. The man. The creepy bad man who'd kidnapped her lay on the ground. He... he wasn't still anymore. He was moving. Twitching. And—and his lips were moving, and his eyes were wide. And—

And then out of nowhere, the two figures appeared. They crouched down, jumped on him, started punching him, started slamming his head against the weed-covered concrete.

And then—and then they did that horrible thing they always did.

They sunk their teeth into his body.

Into his chest.

Tore his T-shirt away, and bit his belly, and ripped the skin and the flesh away, and...

She must've gasped without realising, because Dwayne's hand covered her mouth. The taste of sweat and petrol touched her lips. He held her hand with his warm hand. And for a moment, it was Dad holding her hand, and not Dwayne.

You'll be okay, my girl. You'll be okay.

She breathed in through her nostrils. Then out through the crack in her lips. In. Out. In. Out. Dwayne... Dwayne started pulling her away slightly. Were they moving? Was this their chance to run away?

And then the creepy man on the ground. Suddenly, the bad people weren't on top of him, and he was—he was crawling towards Nisha, and Dwayne, and he was staring right at Nisha with—with anger, spluttering blood, pulling himself towards her like a slug, but a bad slug, a nasty one, not like the nice ones who ate leaves in the garden.

But... but the others. The other two. The ones who'd attacked him.

They were still there.

Still looking at him.

And—and if he kept coming this way, they were going to see her.

They were going to see Dwayne.

The snake tightened around her neck again. Her mouth was so dry. Dwayne's warm hand tightened against hers a little too hard. And then he started to drag her away from the car, away from the creepy man, away from...

And then the two figures looked up at Nisha.

She wanted to believe they weren't looking at her. She wanted to believe they hadn't seen her. She wanted to believe they weren't looking right at her, and that she was invisible because she was still and everything was going to be okay.

Her heart pounded.

The snake tightened.

In.

Out.

In.

Out.

And then the two bad people shot to their feet and raced towards her and Dwayne.

PETE

* * *

Pete held Helen and felt so damned grateful he'd made it home in time.

The clock ticked away in the kitchen, filling the silence. He loved the sound of that clock. He remembered the day Helen brought it home, asked him to put it up. He was on his weekend off, so to say he wasn't best pleased about the prospect of leaving the comfort of the sofa was an understatement. But he got up off the sofa and he put that clock up. It took him way longer than it should've done. He wasn't a DIY whizz, as much as he hated it when Helen pointed it out. He could never get the right drill setting, and on more than one occasion, he'd drilled right through a water pipe, or a live cable.

But when he put that clock up... there was something so soothing about the way it ticked. Sounded ridiculous, he knew. But he loved sitting in that kitchen, with a black coffee, staring out at the garden, watching the birds fly down to the feeders. One of the perks of getting in from night shift. That golden hour. A golden hour of peace. A golden hour of silence. A golden hour of no company at all, but that ticking clock.

He felt Helen's warm body in his arms. The clock ticked away in the kitchen. Outside, the birds sang a beautiful chorus, reminding him of those golden hours. And if he stood here long enough, not thinking, he could convince himself that he was right back there, right back there on one of those mornings, when Helen got up for work, and he gave her a hug before he went upstairs to sleep the day away.

But Helen was crying.

And that dampened the illusion of the old normality, somewhat.

He knew why Helen was crying. He wasn't an idiot. He could *see* the reason Helen was crying, lying right there on the lounge floor. Billy. Her new fella. Blood trickling out of his skull, and all over the hard wood floor. His body, twitching. And looking down at him... it didn't feel real, somehow. He felt like he was in some kind of weird dream. A dream he couldn't wake up from. The enraged pricks outside. The attacks on the motorway. Colin. Stan. And—and that boy. That boy he'd left behind. The boy he swore he'd go back for. The boy he swore he'd save.

And... that violence. The violence he'd shown. Cracking that brick over Billy's head. That level of rage that he was usually so good at suffocating when he was at work; so good at repressing...

So many years of anger, so many years of frustration, so many years of rage, all seeping out of him at that moment.

Helen sobbed in his arms. And all he could do was hold her tight, even though he knew *he* was the reason she was sobbing. "It's okay," he said. "I... I'm here, Helen. We'll—we'll sort this mess out. I'll sort this mess out."

"I want you to leave," she gasped.

Those words hit Pete like a punch to the gut. *I want you to leave*. But—but he'd risked so much to be here with her. He'd sacrificed so much to be here, right now.

"You don't mean that," Pete said.

Helen pushed him away, in an instant. She backed up, into the boundary of the kitchen. Staring at him with those wide eyes. "He —he needs help. Billy needs help."

"Helen, there's—"

"You're not supposed to be here."

"Helen."

"You're supposed—you're supposed to keep your distance from me. That was the agreement. Remember? That's—that's why you can still wear that uniform."

The case.

The solicitors.

The agreement.

Keep his distance from her. Stop "stalking" her. Which was nonsense. He didn't *stalk* her. Tracking her location because the Find Your Friends app was still installed on her phone wasn't stalking. If she didn't want him to know her location at any given time, she could just delete the app, right?

And sure. Turning up at restaurants at the same time as she went on her dates with his replacements probably wasn't the best form. But what rules were stopping him from showing up at dinner at the place she just happened to be?

He took a deep breath of the clammy cottage air. He walked towards her. She backed away from him.

"Helen," he said. Keeping as calm as he could. Raising his hands. "I'm here because you're in danger."

"I don't need your help."

"You haven't seen it out there. You haven't seen what's... what's *happening* out there. The things I've witnessed. The things I've seen. You... If you saw them too, you'd know why it's so important that we stay safe right now."

Helen shook her head. She looked down at Billy's body, then back up at Pete. "I'm not safe. I've never been safe. Not with— not with you."

Shit. Why was she saying this crap again? Making out like he was some kind of controlling monster. They had ten good years of marriage together. Sure, they weren't perfect. Was any marriage? They had their problems. They had their issues. But they worked through them. And they worked through them together.

Until Helen decided she didn't *want* to work through them anymore. Probably because she was already sucking this Billy prick's cock.

Heat filled Pete's face. He had to keep calm. Had to keep his cool. Had to *breathe*.

But he saw the fear in Helen's eyes and it made his stomach sink.

"I'm not a bad person," Pete said.

"You—you've hurt Billy. You've—"

"You don't need to worry about Billy anymore."

"I'm not worried about Billy," Helen cried. "I never *have* been worried about Billy. It's *you* I'm worried about. Get out. Get out of my house. Now."

The audacity. The frigging *audacity.* "*Your* house?"

"Pete, my partner is on the floor. He needs help. Not now—"

"*Your* house?" Pete shouted. His voice echoing against the walls.

"Pete—"

But nothing was stopping him now.

He marched towards Helen. "The last time I checked, Helen, it was still my name on the fucking bills."

"Pete—"

"Because I'm a good man. I'm a good man living in a shitty flat on my own all because I want *you* to be happy."

"You don't want me to be happy," Helen said.

"What?"

"You don't want me to be happy. You just want me to be yours."

Pete stopped. His skin tingled. His heart raced. He saw the

blood on the floor. He heard Stan's screams, and saw the skin peeling away from his face. And he saw that little boy, sitting in the car on the motorway. *"Please don't leave me. Please."*

He saw it all, and he felt that burning anger, right in the pit of his stomach, and it wasn't the woman he loved in front of him. It was someone else entirely. Some*thing* else entirely.

His jaw was clenched tight. His fists, even tighter. He looked into Helen's eyes, and he shook his head.

"Right," he said. "That's how it is. I see how..."

And then he stopped.

Because right behind Helen, right at those glass patio doors, he saw a figure.

A man.

Covered in blood.

Standing there one moment.

Then, racing towards that door.

And smashing into the glass.

KEIRA

* * *

Keira stood at the main entrance to the hospital and her stomach sank, as the two infected raised their heads and looked right at her with those dead eyes.

The infected woman chewed down on a chunk of meat. Blood trickled down her chin, staining her white T-shirt. Her neck was covered with bite wounds. Clear teeth marks. So this was some sort of bite-transmitted disease. Like something from the realm of fiction. Only it wasn't fiction. It was real. And it was happening right now.

A crowd of people hurtled past her and Dad. A chubby man barged into a frail old lady, knocking her to the concrete. A little boy with dark hair ran past, screaming, clinging to his iPad for dear life. An Asian man in a wheelchair desperately dragged himself along, fighting for dear life as the crowd engulfed him.

Keira had to join the crowd, too. She couldn't just stay here. She had to run. Or she was going to die.

But the people. The people on the ground. The people who

needed help. She couldn't just abandon them. She couldn't just leave them...

A tension filled her hand. She looked around. Dad stood there. Wide-eyed. Afraid. "We have to go."

And she wanted to shake her head. She wanted to resist. She didn't want to do what Dad wanted her to do. She didn't want him turning up in her life again after all these years and acting like he was the frigging boss of her; like he had any right to tell her what she should and shouldn't do.

Dad. Dad, being here at all. That was... that was unexpected to say the least. What the hell was he doing here? And as much as there was this part deep inside her that was happy to see him... that part inside made her feel, well, weird. Uncomfortable. She didn't like thinking about Dad too much. She didn't like thinking about the last time she saw him. She didn't like thinking about the decision she made. To turn her back on him.

And she didn't like to think about how he acted after Mum, either.

But right now...

The screaming crowd, whizzing past them.

And the distant movement of the infected, inching closer.

She needed to get out of here.

She needed to go.

She turned around and she ran.

She followed the crowd. Dad and this dog of his ran alongside her. A mother held on to her son, tears streaming down her cheeks. The man in the wheelchair toppled over, spilled right out of it, hit the ground. And people just kept on running. Kept on going, completely possessed with fear.

But Keira... Keira couldn't just leave these people without helping.

She couldn't just leave them.

She ran over to the man who'd fallen from his wheelchair.

Reached down, grabbed his arms. "It's okay. I've got you. Let's—let's get you back up. Let's—"

A sudden thump cracked into Keira's right side.

She tried to stay on her feet, but she collapsed to the concrete, smacking her head against the solid ground.

Ringing filled her ears. The taste of blood filled her mouth. Screaming people raced past her, but they sounded more distant, somehow. Less... focused.

"Keira!" A voice. A distant voice amidst the crowd. Dad.

She looked up.

Dad ran towards her, the dog by his side. His eyes were wide. People banged into him, trying to get away. But Dad didn't even hesitate. He barged past them. Battled through them. Desperately trying to reach her as she lay there on the ground.

She turned around. The man. The man from the wheelchair. He stared at her with wide eyes. Sweat trickled down his bald head, dripping onto the concrete below.

"Please," he gasped. "Pl—ARGH!"

That scream. What—what the hell was that scream? It was a scream of pain. Of agony. It was a scream of...

She looked down to the movement at his legs.

One of those figures.

Sinking their teeth into his right ankle.

Blood spurted up, out from under his jeans, painting the biter —a girl, no older than late teens—square in the face.

"Please!" the man screamed. "Please!"

Keira wanted to help him. She wanted to ease his suffering. She wanted to ease his pain. That—that was her nature. That was her duty in life. That was her purpose.

But—but that biter. And—and more of them. More of them running this way.

She needed to get away.

The man screamed. Shook his head. "Please. Mum. Mum. Please."

And her heart broke for him at that moment. This poor man. This poor soul. Lying face flat on the concrete, right beside her, begging for his mum. The most primal instinct of all.

She shook her head. Started to crawl away. "I'm sorry. I'm—"

The man reached out. Grabbed her. Squeezed her arm. Tight.

She tried to pull her arm away, but she couldn't. He was holding on too tight. Way too tight.

And then the girl who'd bitten him looked up. Right at her. She—she was onto her. She was onto her and she was going to bite her too.

Keira tried to yank her arm away from the screaming man again. "Please. Let—let me go. Let me go!"

The girl's mouth stretched open.

A deathly gasp clawed its way out of her bloodied mouth.

And then she hurtled towards Keira.

DWAYNE

* * *

Dwayne held the kid's hand and watched the infected pricks turn their attention from Pedo Harry to him, and wondered how in the name of Hell he'd got himself caught up in this situation.

The guy on the left dragged himself to his feet and launched himself at Dwayne, waving his arms by his sides.

Panic filled Dwayne's body. He couldn't breathe. He couldn't think. He just had to get up. He just had to run.

He squeezed the kid's hand. Jumped up. And then, holding onto her, he sprinted around the side of Pedo Harry's car, and down the slope towards the road, as fast as he frigging could.

The pursuing infected snarled behind him. And then another desperate cry filled his ears. The other infected. That one was on to him too. Shit. He needed to keep running. Needed to keep bloody going.

He raced down the hill, holding the girl's hand. Shit. Who the hell even was this kid? He shouldn't have got involved. He should've just left her. Whatever problem she'd got herself caught up in wasn't his business.

But then... Pedo Harry. He remembered him well from his time inside. That monster raped kids. And give a man like that a collapsing city like this and an opportunity to act outside the law? Yeah. That shit was a recipe for disaster.

No. He'd done the right thing. He'd done the only thing he could by helping this kid.

But it'd got him into a shitload of bother.

He looked over his shoulder. Both of them. Chasing him. Closer than he thought.

Shit!

He turned back around. The car park gates loomed up ahead. He just had to get onto the street. Find a car. Or—or find a building to hide in. And when he'd hidden in that building, when these infected wankers grew tired of him or bored of trying to find him, he could get out of there and he could focus on his real journey. His actual goal.

Finding Mum.

Getting to her care home.

Getting her out of there—safely.

And whatever happened after that... well, no use in thinking that far ahead right now.

He ran down towards the gates.

And then he stopped.

Smoke rose in the distance, over in the direction of the hospital. Screaming filled the air, constantly hanging in the background from all directions. A woman ran down the road in her blood-drenched dressing gown, screaming. Another woman pursued her. Further up the street, a little boy screamed and slapped his mum's face, splashing blood up all over his hands. "Please wake up, Mummy. Please wake up. Please."

And then, across the road, an older woman.

She had long, grey hair. Wide green eyes. And she stared

intently at Dwayne.

Covered in blood.

And covered in those puncture wounds.

A hand tugged at his. The little girl. Dragging him. Trying to —trying to pull him away.

But Dwayne couldn't move.

His legs were frozen solid to the ground.

The woman. Glaring at him.

Bristol.

"Please don't hurt us. Please—please don't hurt us. Please..."

And the smell of burning and the taste of blood and—

Those snarls, right behind him.

He looked around.

The two infected chasing him and the girl ran towards them both, just metres away.

Crap.

He looked back at the woman across the street. She was running too, now. Running towards him. Hunting him down.

Shit, shit, shit.

So he tightened his grip around the kid's hand and he ran. Ran down the pavement. A sharp pain split through his knee. Those echoing cries of his pursuers closed in. Flames flickered from the houses either side. Sirens and screams filled the air. A car whizzed past, and crashed right into another, as a small mob of people clambered on top of it, smashing the windscreen, desperately trying to get inside, like children trying to crack a Kinder Surprise to find what's inside.

The whole scene was like a crazy VR video game. Or some kind of re-enactment in a messed-up House of Horrors. Only it wasn't a re-enactment. It was real. It was frigging real. And he was caught in the middle of it.

The infected behind him screamed. They were so close. If he slipped or slowed down for a second, he was done. He was finished.

And as much as he wanted to find Mum, as much as he wanted to get to the care home and save her... he had no idea where he was going right now, he had no idea where he was heading, only that he had to keep going. He had to keep running. He had to keep—

An infected appeared right in front of him. Clearly one of them. Big guy. Looked like he'd spilled ketchup all down his front, only it wasn't ketchup. It was blood.

He growled, and then he roared, and then he ran at Dwayne like a rugby player going in for a tackle.

Dwayne froze. But—but no. He couldn't afford to freeze.

He had to keep moving.

But they were approaching behind him.

And to his left.

And up ahead.

That's when he saw the door.

The door, right to his side.

He grabbed that handle and he turned it and—and it opened.

It opened, but...

The kid.

The little girl.

Instinct took over. Sheer instinct, as he looked down at her, saw her terrified, tear-filled eyes.

He couldn't race in the house before her.

He had to let her go first.

So he grabbed her.

He threw her inside, through that door.

And then he threw himself through the door, trying desperately to shut it behind him.

He was halfway through the door when he felt something that made his entire world stand still.

A sharp pain.

Right in the middle of his left forearm.

HELEN

* * *

Helen stared across the kitchen at Pete and wanted this nightmare to end.

He stood there. Stared at her with these wide, bloodshot eyes. She'd... she'd said some pretty rough shit to him just now. She knew that. She didn't even know *what* she'd said, only that it was definitely harsh, but it was also definitely true.

And... and on the floor. On the floor, in the lounge, right behind him. Billy. Her—her partner. Lying there. Bleeding from his skull. Twitching. And—and those sounds. Those choking, gasping sounds he'd let out when Pete first hit him, when he first knocked him to the floor. If this wasn't already a nightmare... then those noises were going to haunt her nightmares.

She wanted to go over to him. She wanted to go over to his side and she wanted to check on him. He—he needed help. He needed an ambulance. He needed seeing to. She—she couldn't just leave him lying there, on the floor. She loved him. She loved him and he needed her right now. He needed her, and...

Pete.

Standing there.

Standing right between her and Billy.

She couldn't remember when she first felt afraid of Pete. They had a pretty average marriage. Until he started shagging other women behind her back. Then trying to justify it to her, claiming *she* was cheating on *him* with every man she dared glance at. Yeah. That was probably the turning point.

But to be honest... she was never afraid of Pete. If anything, he was always pretty pathetic. A coward. Got teased about it at work, too. Last man at the scene of a crime. Do anything to avoid confrontation. And maybe that was a bigger reason why their marriage broke down. Maybe it was that passivity. Maybe it was that lack of confrontation. Maybe, in a way, Helen *wanted* confrontation, because confrontation was the only way they were going to get to the bottom of their issues.

But when Pete confessed to sleeping around... in a way, he became even more pathetic to Helen. He got on his knees and he blubbered for forgiveness. But she didn't feel anything for him. Just pity for him. Total pity.

It was when she went to leave the house that he threw the ashtray at the back of her head. Then immediately apologised for it. Immediately got all *pathetic* about it.

And then the following began.

The stalking. Turning up at places she was at when there was no way he could know she was there. Sometimes, she'd visit random places just to lure him there, just to bait him, just to prove to herself their run-ins weren't just coincidence, they were active cases of stalking.

She found out he was using an app to track her. Something she'd signed up to years ago. Ironically, she could see his location too, so if she'd been privy to it years earlier, she might've caught him in the act of having affairs and cut him loose a whole lot longer ago.

A few months ago, they came to an agreement. Just some bullshit to keep him semi-happy while stopping bloody stalking her at the same time. He could continue to keep his name on the house, but she paid rent to him, something that gave him this weird sense of control over her. But he had to agree to stop stalking her. Or she'd escalate it, legally, and his job would be in jeopardy.

It worked. Or on the surface, it *seemed* to work anyway. It was a stupid idea in hindsight. It gave him way too much power. But... well, it kept him at bay. And *she* had a sense of power, too, over the direction of his job. And she got to keep the house. So there were perks.

So yeah. It worked. Mostly.

But there were days when she sat in coffee shops convinced that eyes were burning into the back of her head.

And right now... on this weird day of chaos, he was here. Right here.

She wanted to get out. But she'd seen the news. The orders to stay inside. The riots, sweeping across cities. Hospitals, falling apart. *Everything* falling apart. It was like lockdown all over again, only even more disorienting, even more confusing. Because at least with COVID, you knew something was coming. The news from overseas. The relative *order* about it.

But with this... with whatever *this* was... things were different.

Especially since the internet seemed to have completely collapsed, and the news channels had gone blank.

Everything had just... disintegrated.

She opened her mouth to tell Pete to piss off out of her house again when suddenly, his eyes widened.

"Helen!"

And then a smash.

A smash, right behind her.

Something—some*one*—flying into her, tackling her to the kitchen floor.

She cracked her forehead on the back of a chair. Went dizzy

instantly, and tasted blood. And then she hit the stone floor with a crack.

Someone—someone was on top of her.

Someone was pinning her down.

Someone was—

She turned around and saw them.

A man. A bald man she didn't recognise. Straddling her. Blood dripping down his chin. Fury in his red, bloodshot eyes.

And... and weird marks on his shoulder.

Like *tooth marks*.

He opened his mouth and moved towards Helen when suddenly a crack split through the air.

Pete.

Pete, dragging that man off her.

Wrestling him to the floor.

And then punching him. Punching him, hard. Battering him. Beating him into the stone floor.

She watched Pete thump this man in the head, again and again. And she saw the repressed anger in his eyes, flooding out. And as blood splattered up all over him... she realised there wasn't much different between him and this—this attacker, whoever he was, after all.

She watched him and she looked back at Billy. Lying there. Still. She needed to go over to him. She needed to check on him. She needed to help him.

But...

The windows. The patio windows.

A chance.

A chance to get away from Pete.

Because even though the news said it was dangerous outside... it was dangerous *inside*, too.

She didn't want to leave Billy behind. She'd come back for him. Really, she would.

But right now, she needed to get away from here.

Where to?

Anywhere.

Anywhere but here.

She went to get up to her feet as her head spun and her body shook when she saw Pete staring down at her.

He was covered in blood.

But he was looking right down at her.

Holding out his hand to her.

"It's okay," he said, grabbing her hand. Gently pulling her to her feet. "You're going to be okay now, honey. Everything's going to be okay."

And then he pulled her in to his arms again, and she saw the open patio windows behind her, the sharp broken glass, and Helen had never felt more trapped—or more afraid—in her entire life.

DAVID

* * *

D avid watched the girl drag herself off the disabled man
and lunge towards Keira, and in that instant, his whole
world stood still.

The girl threw herself at Keira, who lay there, on the ground.
More people ran past. Screaming. Shouting. Desperately trying to
escape the oncoming group of... infected people? Was that what
they were? That's what it looked like, anyway. Shit. He didn't
know what the hell was going on. Just that this was no normal
riot. He could tell that from Mrs Kirkham alone, and her nurse.
Take the shitshow at the hospital out of the equation completely
and it was still pretty damned clear something was happening.
Something big.

But this girl. Flying towards Keira. Flying towards his daughter. Towards his girl.

He watched her, frozen, in slow motion, and he saw Rina.

Rina. In the middle of the road. The shouting. The crying.
The screaming.

"David, help. Please. Please help. Please!"

And he felt that same heaviness, in his legs.

He felt that same iciness, running through his veins. That same sense of being stuck. Being stuck knee deep in tar, sinking, unable to move a muscle.

And that same sense of guilt...

"Please, David. Help. Help us. Please..."

And then he saw this girl and he saw Keira and he saw an opportunity, he saw a chance.

He ran towards the girl. Body slammed her, even though it went against every instinct in his body. She—she wasn't normal. She was filled with rage. And even though it felt wrong... all he knew was that if this girl got Keira, if he bit her, by the looks of things, Keira would catch whatever crazy virus was spreading, too.

And he'd do anything to protect his girl.

He pushed the infected girl back. Right against the ground. Hard.

She looked up. Not really *at* him, but in his general direction. Like a horsefly, swatted away, disoriented from its prey.

And then... and then this infected girl's attention turned to someone else. Someone else in the crowd. She ran at this other person. And—and David felt guilty. David felt sad. Because—because this girl. She was going to attack someone else. Someone else was going to suffer the same fate that he'd just rescued Keira from. Someone else's daughter. Someone else's *Keira*.

But he couldn't dwell on that. Not right now.

He turned around, back to where Keira was. Saw her, still lying there. The man... the man who'd fallen out the wheelchair. Bleeding. Spluttering. Keira, crouched over him. "It's okay. You're going to be okay. I'm here. I'm—I'm here."

The man lay there. Blood seeping out the corners of his mouth. Choking. Gasping. But amidst the chaos, Keira was an island of calm for this man. She was there for him. By his side. Exactly what he needed right now.

He wanted to get out of here. This hospital, it wasn't safe

here. The hospital itself was a towering inferno at this point. Not a fire engine in sight. People racing past each other. Screaming. Shouting. He needed to get away from this hellscape. But... but in a way, he didn't want to tear Keira away from this man right now. It looked so natural, what she was doing. Looking after him. Caring for him.

But they had to go.

He put a hand on Keira's shoulder. "Keira."

Keira flinched. She turned around, just a little, then looked back down at the man, spluttering on the ground. "You'll be okay. Ssh. I'm here. I'm—I'm here."

David looked up. Saw a man ripping a chunk out of a woman's shoulder. Another man wrestling an old bloke to the ground, biting into his belly. And... and at the back of the crowd, another one of these infected people clutched on to their bleeding neck, and twitched around on the ground. Almost like the adrenaline-fuelled rage they were charged up with had run out, and they were finally succumbing to their injuries. A nightmare. A total out-of-body experience. One he couldn't understand. One he couldn't comprehend.

He saw Rufus, tail between his legs, panting.

He looked back down at Keira. "Keira, we really need to go."

But Keira still wasn't looking. Keira still wasn't listening. She was still holding this man's hand. Still comforting him.

Up ahead, by the hospital doors, David heard a scream. He looked up. Two more people covered in flames, racing out of the entrance area, swinging their arms around in a combination of agonised pain and enraged frenzy. What the hell was happening? What the hell even was this?

He looked back down at Keira. And as much as she was trying her best to be there for this man right now... David saw his daughter right in front of him—a daughter he'd lost once in his life already—and he wasn't willing to let her die because of his passivity.

So he took a deep breath.

And as much as he didn't like the thought of it—as much as he knew Keira wasn't going to appreciate it—he dragged her to her feet.

"Hey! Get off! Get—"

"We're going," he said.

"Get off me!"

And then he turned around, held her arm tight, and he dragged his daughter away; away, with Rufus; away from the crowd, away from the chaos, and away into whatever disarray awaited ahead...

NISHA

* * *

Nisha tumbled onto the hallway floor and knew she had to get up—right away.

The taste of blood filled her mouth. Her heart wouldn't stop racing. She felt dizzy, and she felt sick, and her legs felt like they were covered in ice, which was getting colder and colder, harder and harder.

But she couldn't just lie here.

She had to get up.

She had to get away.

She turned around and she saw the man who'd saved her, Dwayne, right there at the door. He was trying to push it back. But—but his arm was bleeding. Blood, trickling right out of his arm, as he pressed back against that door, as he tried to stop the bad people behind from breaking in. Nisha saw their arms, pushed right through the open crack at the side of the door. There were so many of them. Like there was one big monster behind that door, with many arms, and it was going to break that door down and gobble up everything inside.

But... that blood.

She saw that blood and she thought of Beth. The teeth marks. The teeth marks she didn't want to ask Beth about. The teeth marks she didn't want to know about. Because—because she didn't want to think about what those teeth marks meant. She wanted Beth to be her friend. Her best friend. Her only friend.

But then... but then she saw what happened to Beth. She saw her... change. Drop to the road, shake around, blood spurting everywhere, then she changed.

She changed into someone who didn't like Nisha. Someone who hated Nisha. Someone like... someone like everyone else.

She saw that blood again now. Blood, oozing from Dwayne's arm. What if the same thing happened to him? What if he changed, just like Beth had changed? Just like Mrs Thompson changed? Just like *everyone* had changed?

She closed her burning eyes and she thought about Beth and the blood and—and the kids at school and Ginger Harry and—

And then she thought of Dad.

Dad. Where would he be right now? He'd—he'd be at home. He'd be at home, worrying about her. Only... No. Dad would've gone to school to find her. Because he loved her. He loved her and he would've done anything for her.

But...

But she'd run away from school. Because it wasn't safe there. Even though it was bad to run away from school, it wasn't safe there, so she'd done what she had to do. She'd done the only thing she could.

She saw the man, Dwayne, pushing back against the door. Holding those people back—those angry flailing arms back.

She looked over her shoulder. Saw a dark corridor. Saw a staircase. Saw a kitchen at the back of the house. A kitchen she could escape through. A kitchen she could run out the back door through and then—and then search for home. Find her home and then find Dad and then everything was going to be good, everything was going to be okay, everything was going to be...

But then she remembered this man. Dwayne.

Saving her. Saving her from the bad man's car.

Saving her from that car and then bringing her here and now pushing that door closed as hard as he could and...

Her stomach sank. She—she had a chance to run. A chance to go. A chance to get away.

And she was scared. She was so scared. Her face burned hot. Her heart kept beating fast in her chest, pounding and pounding. And she couldn't move. She felt... she felt stuck. Stuck to the floor, like there was a carpet of glue underneath her, holding her down, dragging her down.

She saw the look on Dwayne's face. Saw his wide eyes. Saw his body, shaking, as he tried to hold the monsters back.

And then she took a deep breath.

She thought of what Dad would say to her right now.

Be strong. Do the right thing.

She got up. Dragged herself to her feet. And even though she wanted to run, even though she wanted to get away... she knew what she had to do.

She knew the right thing to do.

She ran.

Ran towards the door.

Ran towards the man.

His eyes widened. His lips moved. Like he was saying something to her. Trying—trying to speak to her.

But she couldn't hear.

So she ran up to that door and she ran up to his side and she pressed her back against the door, too.

She stood there. Stood there and felt the door shaking. Even though they were pressing against it, even though they were trying to block the bad people from getting in, the door was moving. It—it was opening. The bad people. They were going to get in.

She looked up at Dwayne. He looked down at her. Wide-eyed. He wasn't saying anything. He was... he was just looking at her. This scared look in his eyes. Like he'd just seen a monster.

She looked at the blood on his arm. Then back up at him. He shook his head. His lips moved. She didn't see what he was saying, she couldn't tell, but his lips were moving and she was terrible at lipreading and—and she wanted to imagine he was telling her to run. Telling her to go.

Do the right thing, angel.

She turned around. Stared down the corridor. Tears streaming down her face. Her feet moved in front of her as she tried to hold back the door, as she tried to be strong, as she tried to do the right thing.

Just do the right thing, angel. Do the right thing...

She thought of Dad.

Thought of his smile.

Thought of the touch of his fingers in her hair as he stroked her head to sleep.

And then she thought of how proud he would be of her, of knowing how strong she was, how strong she had been.

Do the right thing.

Do the...

And then the door flew forward, and Nisha tumbled face flat to the hard hallway floor.

PETE

* * *

Pete looked down at Helen as she crouched sobbing by the side of her "partner," and he wasn't sure what to feel.

So Billy was dead. Which... didn't exactly surprise Pete. He'd hit him over the head. Then—then he'd kept on hitting him; hitting him and hitting him as hot blood splattered up over his hands, as sharp shards of exposed skull split through his knuckles.

And... and he couldn't explain the emotion inside him right now. He felt like he was in some sort of cloud. Some sort of... bubble. His emotions, his feelings, everything, they all felt like they were happening some place *outside* of him. Some distant place, which he could see quite clearly, but which didn't feel like they were happening to *him* directly.

He knew he should feel guilty. He knew he should feel bad about what he'd done.

But truth be told, Pete didn't feel anything of the sort.

Pete looked down at the bloody mush that remained of Billy's face. Blood. Muscle. Cracked skull. Brain. And Helen. Lying there beside him. Muttering to him.

And... and it made him feel weird. It *irked* him. Because Helen was his wife for the longest time. And this was *his* home. So she had no damned right moping and sulking about some bastard replacement.

And in a way, in time... Pete saw this as the perfect opportunity. It was a chance. A chance to be here for her, when she needed him most. A chance to be the *only* person here for her. It might sound sinister. But this tragic death might just be the best thing that ever happened to the pair of them. Because it was going to bring them back together. It was going to heal their wounds. It was going to—

"I hate you."

Those words. Those words from Helen's lips. Those naive words. They made him roll his eyes a bit. Because she was in shock. She was grieving, or whatever. Sure. She had to deal with this shit in her own time.

But... in time, she would get there. In time, she would conquer this.

And he was going to be right here to help her get through it all.

He looked across the kitchen. Over at the second man, lying dead on their kitchen floor. The violence of the streets was spreading here, out in the countryside. He thought about Stan. He thought about Colin. He thought about the blood. And he knew something *wrong* was happening. Something sincerely, seriously *wrong* was going down.

The bites. It looked like it was in the bites. Or the blood. Something like that. He'd seen so many signs that it was violence itself that spread this... this virus? This disease? Whatever the hell it was.

He thought about the man lying on the kitchen floor. He thought about Billy, lying there, Helen perched above him. Did *he* have whatever disease was spreading across the city like wildfire? He wasn't sure. It was hard to tell. Hard to know. Did even the infected people know themselves?

He had no idea.

He just knew that his sole purpose was right on the floor in front of him.

Helen. Crying. Sobbing.

He wanted to comfort her. He wanted to reassure her. He wanted to tell her she was going to be okay. That everything was going to be okay. Because it was. It really was. He was going to make sure of that.

He reached down. Put a hand on her shoulder. Felt the warmth of her body searing through the softness of her shirt.

"It's okay, Helen. I'm here. I've got you. I've—"

She jumped up. Grabbed him, right around the throat. Sunk her nails so deep into his neck that it actually hurt. She pushed him back, pressed her face right up against his. Her eyes bulged, bloodshot. But she wasn't infected. Not like the others. She... she was very much her. She was just angry. So angry.

"You killed him," she gasped.

"Helen," Pete coughed, choking. "I—"

"You—you killed him. You violent, violent man. You killed him, and you think I'd want you here? You think I'd want *anything* to do with you? After what—after what you've done?"

Pete forced a deep gulp. He reached up with his shaking, blood-soaked hands. And then he dragged her arms away. Held her tenderly. But moved those arms with force.

He dragged them away. Pushed them against Helen's chest, hard. And then he held her there with one hand, then covered her mouth with his other hand, pushing her back against the wall.

The anger in her eyes shifted, somewhat. That anger... changed.

That anger morphed from pure anger into... something like fear.

"Here's how things are going to go," Pete said.

Helen tried to move her lips beneath his palm, but she couldn't.

"You're going to let me take your little plaything into the garden and bury him. And then I'm going to board up the patio windows. And while whatever shit is going down outside... we're going to lay low and we're going to stay here. Together."

Helen's eyes twitched. Anger in those eyes. Hatred.

"And we have two choices. Either we can try and get along. Or... or we can make this far, far more difficult than it has to be. What's it going to be?"

A tear trickled down her face.

For a moment, Pete felt the strength from that dominance. The strength from that sense of power.

And then he pulled his hand away.

Helen gasped. She keeled over, spluttered all over the floor, dry heaving.

Pete leaned down. Patted her back, gently. "That's right," he said. "You get it all up. You've been through quite a shock. Quite a change. Both of us have. I'm sorry. I'm so, so sorry."

And then he stroked her hair.

Felt a warmth, deep inside.

And in the midst of the blood, and the death, and the horror, a smile crept up his face.

"We're going to be okay," he said. "You're going to be okay. I'm going to look after you. Everything's going to be okay."

KEIRA

* * *

Keira couldn't stop looking over her shoulder at the burning remains of the hospital and thinking about all the people she knew and loved, still trapped in those flames, scrambling for their lives.

The sky was grey. Hard to tell whether that was from the cloud or from the smoke. The streets were in ruin. Abandoned cars littered the roads. Supermarkets pulled down their shutters, desperately scrambling to keep the outside world away. All around, dogs barked and howled. People screamed. Keira could hear a woman somewhere over the back of Booths, in those houses. "Mark! Please wake up. Please wake up!"

And her pain. Her anguish. Just hearing those words... it brought it all home. The loss. The chaos. The sense of crisis, rapidly spreading, just like wildfire.

It was pretty damned clear that this wasn't just confined to the hospital. This was... this was far, far wider than that. Far bigger than that.

The smell of smoke filled her nostrils. Every now and then,

she found herself coughing, spluttering, that smoke inhalation from when she was trapped inside the hospital making her gag. She was so lucky. So fortunate to make it. Out. So lucky to survive. But in a way, now she was out... processing everything she'd witnessed, everything she'd been through, a part of her wondered whether getting out and escaping was such a good thing after all.

She heard footsteps beside her. Turned around in this spaced-out haze and saw Dad. Walking by her side. Focused on the road ahead. His eyes were wide, too. He looked like he was also in a kind of haze. Walking here, beside her, with this Golden Retriever dog. When the hell did he decide to get a dog? The dog didn't exactly look like a pup, either. And as far as she remembered, Dad was hardly the *rescuing* type.

She looked at Dad and she felt this burning in the pit of her stomach. He'd turned up at the hospital. He'd dragged her away when she was trying to help someone. He shouldn't have done that. Who the hell did he think he was, doing that? Because—because she hadn't seen him in years. She hadn't seen him in years, and he couldn't just barge right in and start making decisions like that on her behalf.

He looked around at her, and he half-smiled, like a kid who knew he'd misbehaved.

"You shouldn't have dragged me away from there. You had—you had no right."

Dad's face turned. "What?"

"The hospital. That's... that's where I work. And it's my job to care for people. To look after people."

"I was helping you."

"There was someone who needed help."

"If I hadn't dragged you away, you'd be dead."

"And that wasn't your decision to make," Keira snapped.

Dad opened his mouth. Then closed it. The dog—Rufus, apparently—looked between them and whined.

"Look," Keira said, her head absolutely banging. "I don't know what's happening here. Not really. But... but I do know there's something I need to do."

"Yeah. What you need to do is come home with me so we can lock the doors and ride this out, however long it lasts."

Keira felt her eyes narrowing. "Erm. No. That's not what I meant."

"Keira—"

"I have a friend. *Had* a friend. I... I made a promise to that friend. A promise that I'd... that I'd find a little girl. A little girl who needs help right now. A little girl who is so alone right now. And I can't just abandon her. I can't just leave her. Not... not while things are this bad."

Dad shook his head. "You've seen how it is. Look at the streets. They're—they're not safe."

"And neither is hiding at home," Keira said. "And it's certainly not safe for a kid. On her own. So I... I need to find her. I can't just leave her. It's just not something I'm willing to do."

Dad rubbed his fingers across his forehead, and through his greasy hair. He looked tired. Tireder than Keira remembered. Like life had knocked the wind out of his sails. "This kid. Where is she?"

"That's the thing," Keira said. "I don't really know."

"You don't really know?"

"I know where her dad lived. Omar. I know where he lived. If I can get to his place, I can see if she's there. And if she isn't... I can find what school she's at. And go there."

"And then what?"

"What?"

"You find this kid. Then what?"

Keira shook her head. Then what? It was a good point. She didn't know. She didn't have a clue what came next. Instinctively, she hoped it would just be a case of waiting things out before the army dealt with whatever shit was unfolding.

But looking at the scenes around her, she was beginning to wonder whether that was a possibility at all.

"Well whatever you decide, I'm coming with you."

A knot tightened in Keira's chest. "What?"

"You heard me. I know how stubborn you can be."

"Charming."

"And I know you're not going to change your mind."

"True."

"And even though I think it's absolutely crazy considering the circumstances... I'm not letting you do this alone."

Keira shook her head. "I—I'd rather do this alone—"

"You might be stubborn, Keira. But don't forget who you got that from."

Keira turned away. She didn't want to look at him. She didn't want his jokes. She didn't want to see him smile right now.

She just turned around and tried to think up another reason not to have Dad join her on this journey.

"Dad, really. I'd rather—"

"You can say whatever you want. I'm not letting you do this alone, Keira. So feel free to waste your energy arguing. It's pointless."

Keira shook her head. Looked back at Dad. And as much as she didn't want him here, as much as she wanted to resist, as much as she wanted to *hate* the thought of him joining her... she kind of felt sorry for him. And that made her feel even worse.

She felt her walls collapsing, as she looked at him. She felt herself remembering the good days in the past. The good days in her childhood. The happy memories. The laughter. The closeness. The warmth. The togetherness.

And then she remembered Mum—what happened to Mum—and those walls shot right up again.

"You can come with me, if you have to," Keira said.

Dad smiled. "Seen sense, I see—"

"But this doesn't mean things are back to normal between us."

Dad's face turned. "What—"

"We find Omar's daughter. And then when we find her, and when we've got her to safety, and when... and when everything is back to normal... we go our separate ways again."

She saw his face drop. Saw him turn pale. She saw him open his mouth to try to say something, to try to protest.

And then she took a deep breath, and she turned around, and carried on walking.

She felt a knot in her throat, tightening, tightening

Tears stinging her eyes.

She wished things could be different.

She wished things could be normal.

But they couldn't.

They couldn't ever be normal, ever again.

DWAYNE

* * *

Dwayne felt the sharp pain in his arm and his first thought was: oh fucking fuck, they got me.

He spun around. Looked at his arm, where a splitting pain currently shot through. They'd got him. The infected had got him. They bit each other. That's what they did. That's how whatever the hell this was spread. He'd seen it in Nico. And Nico had been bitten, too. He'd seen so much of this shit in such a short space of time already. And now he was bitten, and he wasn't going to be able to get to the care home in time, which meant he wasn't going to be able to get to Mum in time.

But when he turned around to the source of that stinging... it wasn't what he expected.

A woman. A woman with long fingernails. False nails, by the looks of things. Digging them right down into his arm, splitting his flesh.

A momentary relief. He—he wasn't bitten. He wasn't bitten, which meant he wasn't infected, which meant he was going to be okay. For now at least, he was going to be okay. And those nails were false, too, so if this virus spread any other way then he should be safe from plastic nails, right?

But then he saw more of those figures. More infected. More of them, flying towards this door, which he desperately tried to close in time.

He pushed it back. Slammed it shut as hard as he could. Pressed his back to it.

And then he saw the girl.

She was lying there in front of him. Staring up at him. And—and he realised she was the reason he was here. If he'd just left her... he wouldn't be in this mess. If he'd just left her and not stuck his damned nose in, then he could be well on his way to finding Mum right now, to saving her, to getting her out of that care home and getting her to safety—wherever safety was.

But...

He remembered seeing Pedo Harry taking her into his car. And... and he knew he would never have been able to live with himself if he'd just left her to him. Pedo Harry was a monster. And a Pedo Harry in a world in chaos? That bastard was going to be worse than ever.

But now... now, he was here, struggling to hold back a door of these—these whatever the hell they were, snarling, growling, banging against the door, and all because of this girl.

"Go," he muttered. "You should—you should go. Run. While you can."

But she just stared at him. Deaf. She was deaf. He'd realised that much. She couldn't speak. She was deaf and he didn't know a damned thing about sign language. And he couldn't exactly write right now. He had to... he had to just hope she understood. Because as shitty as it was right now... the best thing she could do to honour his inevitable sacrifice was to get the hell away.

"Go," Dwayne said. "Get the hell out of here. While you still can."

The door banged. Creaking on its hinges. Deafening gasps echoed from behind, and into this dark, murky hallway.

"Go," he mumbled. "Just... just get up and..."

And then she stood. She stood, and she looked over her shoulder. And for a second, for just a second, she looked like she was going to turn around and run. Which was what she needed to do. She needed to get out of here. She needed to save herself.

But then something remarkable happened.

She ran in his direction.

"Oh, shit," he said, his stomach sinking. "Kid. What're you doing? What're you..."

And then she stood at the door. Pushed back against it. Stood right beside him, and tried to hold this growing mass of raging people back.

She looked up at him. And he looked down at her. And at this moment, this silent moment amidst all the chaos... he felt like she was thanking him. Like this poor young girl was saying thank you for helping her. And this was her way of thanking him.

A knot tightened in his throat.

His eyes started to sting.

She couldn't be here. She couldn't stay here. She couldn't...

And then she slipped, and the door opened, and...

Dwayne tumbled over. He grabbed the kid. He spun around and he saw the enraged figures, standing there. A man with dark hair and wearing a hi-vis, blood seeping out from his eyes. The woman with the false nails, all dolled up, the clear markings of a bite wound on her throat.

All of them in the corridor.

All of them in this building.

And as far as Dwayne could tell... only one way to go.

"Come on!" he said, grabbing the girl's hand. "Quick!"

And then he ran. He ran, holding her hand. But—but she wasn't moving so well after the fall. She was limping along. Limping along and not moving quickly enough. Shit. Oh shit.

He ran through to the kitchen, slamming the door on his way. It only took a few seconds for the door to bang as the infected slammed into it. The back door. Out the back door, out of this house, then over the fence, take a frigging breather, and then to the care home. Than to find Mum. Then...

He grabbed the handle to the back door.

The handle didn't budge.

He looked at the girl. The girl looked up at him. Wide-eyed. She moved her lips. Mumbled something inaudible. And then waved. Like she was trying to tell him something trying to point to something.

All the while, the kitchen door banging, banging...

And then Dwayne reached into his pocket with his shaking hand. Pulled out the pad and pen. Dropped it to the floor. Went to pick it up, but the kid got there first. She crouched down. Wrote something, her hands shaking. What was she writing? What was she...

And then he saw it.

One word.

Window.

He turned around.

The window above the kitchen sink was open. It was small, but it was open. He had no idea how he was going to get out. He had no idea whether he was going to fit.

But he had to try.

He had to frigging try.

He went to lift the girl up so she could get out first when something made him freeze.

The kitchen door.

It slammed open.

And a crowd of angry, bite-covered and blood-drenched pursuers poured right into the kitchen.

HELEN

* * *

Helen watched Pete boarding up the patio windows and couldn't move a muscle.

She was... frozen. She felt like she was dreaming. Like—like she was trapped in a dream. An awful dream. A nightmare. The bodies on the floor. The body of the man she didn't know—the man who'd flown in through the patio windows, attacked her. And then the body of... the body of Billy.

Lying there.

Lying on the wooden floor.

Blood seeping out of his broken, distorted face.

She looked down at Billy and she wanted to vomit. She looked down at Billy and she wanted to *cry*. Because—because she loved him. He wasn't the most exciting man in the world, but she loved him. He wasn't the most caring man in the world at times, but she loved him—and she loved him dearly.

She looked down at Billy and she imagined being in bed with him. Being beside him. Lying there, in his big, strong arms, and for a moment, for just a moment, thinking everything was okay. Truly believing that everything was going to be okay.

And now he was mush.

Mush, on the wooden floor.

Gone.

Gone forever.

She felt... cold. She couldn't even process what she was looking at when she looked at his broken head. She couldn't wrap her head around it. And even though she *tried* to, it still didn't make sense to her. Almost as if she wasn't *supposed* to understand it. Like the mind filtered the most horrible things from comprehension.

Or maybe she was just in shock. Maybe she was just... lost in this shocked haze.

She looked up at Pete. Saw him boarding that broken patio glass up. He said he was going to deal with Billy's body first. But— but these people outside. These angry people, suddenly attacking everyone. Apparently, protecting "their home" from them was more important.

She watched Pete boarding up that glass and she was convinced he'd lost his mind. She knew he had a temper. That was no surprise to her. She didn't know about it for the most years. He was always such a coward. Always so soft. And that was one of the reasons they ended up separating, in the end. Why she was attracted elsewhere. He never challenged her. He wasn't assertive enough. He wasn't... *dominant* enough. And call it a character flaw, but Helen loved dominant.

But one day, he flipped. He threw an ash tray at her. Slung it right at her. And then he launched towards her, anger in his eyes, and gripped her throat, staring into her eyes with those big, bloodshot, angry eyes.

And then he broke down and apologised to her, like a wreck.

They separated. They went their different ways. They came to an agreement—an agreement that would let him keep his job, and let her keep the house.

But... the chaos outside. The panic in the streets. The mass confusion. She'd tried turning the television on, but there was just an emergency broadcast running—an emergency broadcast urging them to stay at home, to lock their doors, to close their curtains. Like the COVID lockdown announcement, but on steroids: more rolling news, less Boris Johnson.

And she'd tried ringing the police. But she couldn't get through. She *actually* couldn't get through to the 999 emergency line. If ever there was a sign that shit wasn't good, then there it was, right there.

She looked out the front window. Nobody out there. The hedge, opposite, leading to the fields. She could run. Run into the fields. Run into the fields they always used to walk Willow. Run across those fields, run down the bridleway, and run up to the farm. John, the farmer, he was a good guy. He'd let her in. He'd let her hide there. Let her lay low there for a while. And if he didn't... well, she'd find somewhere else to run. Somewhere else to hide.

She looked back into the kitchen and she saw Pete. Whistling. And it made the hairs on her arms stand on end. He was actually *whistling* to himself while he worked. Which seemed absolutely absurd. Completely bizarre. He was whistling to himself while he worked, right after... right after beating Billy to death. And killing another man, by the looks of things. One of the infected people.

He turned around. Looked right at her. He smiled at her, just like he used to when he was doing any sort of manual job. That "don't worry, honey, I've got this" expression to his smug face.

And it convinced Helen that he'd lost his mind. Seeing him there, blood splattered across his arms and flecks of it on his face, he looked like a man who'd gone crazy. A man who'd lost it. A man whose grip on reality had well and truly slipped.

She smiled back at him. Because right now, it felt like the safest thing to do.

And then he turned around. Started banging at the wooden board covering the smashed patio windows.

And Helen knew what she had to do.

She turned around and she ran towards the living room door, then towards the porch door, and then towards the front door of the cottage and she could taste freedom, she could sense escape, she could *feel* it, edging closer, and—

And then she felt something.

Tightening, right around her ankle.

Sending her tumbling to the floor. Face flat.

She slammed against the floor. Tasted blood. Shit. She'd— she'd fallen over, and she needed to get back to her feet, and—

Breath. Heavy breathing, right against her neck.

A hand, around her throat.

And a voice that sent a shiver right down Helen's spine.

"Where do you think you're going?"

DAVID

* * *

David and Keira walked down the street towards this "Omar's" place and David wanted nothing more than to get off the streets and get home to safety.

Or something *resembling* safety, anyway.

Clouds covered the afternoon sky. Was it afternoon? Or was it late morning? Hard to tell at this point. He was losing track. He felt... hot. Sweaty. Although a ton of that was most likely the stress and the adrenaline of everything.

This street he was on was similar to the bulk of other streets he'd been on. The main road, the A6, leading right through the heart of Preston. It was usually busy. Usually bustling. Too busy and bustling, to an extent.

Only right now, it was a very different kind of busy and bustling.

Cars lined the sides of the road. Some of the drivers hadn't even bothered parking up—they'd just abandoned their cars, right in the middle of the street. Some of those cars hadn't been abandoned. People sat inside. Men, gripping their steering wheels. Or curled up in the back of the car, desperately tapping at their phones for some kind of news, some kind of reassurance from the great god of the internet. So many smashed windows. And in the distance, that constant hum of screaming.

He thought about the infected. The people. Biting each other. And then... people turning into these rage-fuelled monsters, some of them within a matter of seconds; others, a little longer. Was there any other way this virus spread? Could it spread through cuts and bruises? Or saliva, blood, bodily fluids? He wasn't sure. He didn't have a damned clue.

And he wasn't keen on finding out.

"You happy we didn't drive now?" David asked.

Keira glanced around at him, then back at the road. She was so focused, so clearly determined. She always was so focused when she wanted something. Didn't matter whether it was passing a school test or trying to convince him and Rina to buy her an Xbox at Christmas—being the gamer girl she always used to be— when she had her heart and her mind set on something, she was impossible to bargain with.

But that obsession and that determination had the potential to be dangerous. And right now, David could see that danger first-hand—the dangerous ramifications, the harsh consequences.

He smelled smoke. He heard sirens. Where the hell *were* all the police anyway? Surely the police should be helping control this situation right now. And what about the army? That was always the way in the movies and on the TV shows, right? The army always swooped in to save the frigging day, without fail.

So where were they now?

"We should really head—"

"Don't say 'home'," Keira said.

David felt his jaw tense. It hurt him, honestly. He just wanted to reconnect with Keira. He had this opportunity, right in front of him, to do things differently. They'd been thrown into this crisis together. And what were they doing? How were they acting? Well,

Keira still seemed like she didn't want anything to do with him. Almost like his very presence was an inconvenience.

"So this... this whatever the hell it is. What do you think's happening?"

Keira looked around at him, as Rufus walked between them. "Are you trying to small talk?"

"I saw... I saw an old woman with a broken leg launch herself at me and try to kill me. I saw her nurse try to do the same thing."

"And I saw my best workmate get torn apart, right in front of me," Keira said. "Right after I saw—right after I saw the dad of the kid I'm trying to find launch at another colleague. So forgive me if... forgive me if I don't seem mad keen on talking about it right now."

David's stomach sank. "I'm sorry. For what—for what you've had to witness."

Keira shook her head. "Yeah, well, I'll deal with it. In my own head."

That was classic Keira. Bottle her problems. Repress them and crawl away from them, until the day they finally blew up and exploded.

"The people," David said. "With the bites. I saw... I saw one of them keel over. Clutching his throat."

"Right."

"It's almost as if... it's almost as if these people forget how wounded they are for a while. Like they—like they power on through the pain, or whatever. But eventually... eventually, their wounds catch up with them. Kill them."

"Okay."

"A wound to the neck might be fatal, eventually. But a wound to an arm or something? That... that could last a whole lot longer."

Keira didn't say anything. And David realised he really was just getting carried away in theory and speculation. Truth was, he didn't know. Nobody knew. And that was scary. Really damned scary.

"Well if we aren't gonna talk about this—this *virus* or whatever it is, then you can at least talk to me a little bit about your life."

"My *life?*" Keira said.

"Yeah. Your life. If you've got one. If not, no offence intended."

Keira shook her head. "My life's fine."

"And that's it?"

"What do you want me to say? That my life is shit and I'm missing you terribly?"

"Keira..."

"Look," Keira said. "I... I'm alright, okay?"

"You got a boyfriend?"

"Why does that matter?"

"Because I'm interested. I tried... I tried calling you. Texting you. But I... I couldn't get through."

She looked at him. Held eye contact with him for a few seconds. Then sighed. "I don't have a boyfriend, no."

"Good. One less problem to worry about today. You live alone?"

"With friends."

"Friends. That's good. Living alone's no good. Well, it's alright for a few days. And then it gets... lonely. And then before you know it you realise you're kind of content with it. Kind of okay with it. And that's when the problems really hit. 'Cause at that point... you're kind of a prisoner of your own mind. And nothing on the outside compares to staying in."

Keira looked at him for a few seconds. Held eye contact with him. And he could see the hurt in her eyes. He could see a semblance of *pain* in her eyes.

"I do miss you, you know?" he said. "After... after Mum. After what happened. I just wanted to make things... right."

Her eyes widened. He could see tears building in them, and

they looked bloodshot. She opened her mouth, like she was going to say something, like she was going to open up, like she was going to connect. And he could sense her getting closer. He could sense himself getting closer to her. He could sense their wounds healing.

She moved her lips and went to speak when suddenly, David heard something, right behind him.

A screech of tires.

A deafening scream.

And then a series of skin-crawling snarls.

NISHA

* * *

Nisha stood at the kitchen window and watched the bad people all run through the kitchen door, towards Dwayne.

When she saw them, she felt so scared. She—she couldn't move. She couldn't even think. Everything was in slow motion. She felt time standing still. She felt like she was watching it on a screen and it was all moving so slowly. Except it wasn't happening on a screen. It was happening for real. And it was happening right in front of her.

The bad people all looked angry. She could see their mouths moving. And even though she couldn't hear them, she could imagine they were shouting. Shouting and screaming so loud.

Dwayne stood by the sink. He stared at the men and the woman as they got closer to him. And—and she felt bad. She felt so bad. Because there was no door there now that she could help him hold back. There was just... him.

And how was she supposed to protect him now?

She turned around quickly and saw the window. The open window. It was small. But—but she could get out of there. And maybe Dwayne could get out of there too. It was going to be a tight squeeze. But if he hurried, if he got up here fast, he could try.

She looked back round.

The first bad man—dressed in a police outfit—ran across the kitchen, threw himself over the table. The others followed him. Desperate to get over that table. Desperate to get to Dwayne.

And she wanted to run. She wanted to get away. She felt like she'd felt in that corridor: like there was no time left, and she was scared, and she wanted to get home to Dad because Dad would know what to do and Dad would make everything okay.

But if she ran... this man who'd helped her would get torn up, right in front of her.

But there was nothing she could do for him. Nothing she could do to help him.

She stood there on the edge of the sink and she felt herself getting all shaky and her eyes stinging and she knew what she had to do.

She went to take a step back when she remembered something.

Mrs Thompson.

The toilets.

Holding her back. Pinning her against the wall.

And then...

And then dropping her.

Letting her go.

And it didn't make sense. It didn't make sense at the time. And she hadn't had the time to think about it much since.

But Mrs Kirkham had let her go.

What if...

No. She didn't have time. She didn't have the time to try

anything. She didn't have the time to mess around. She needed to climb out that window. And she needed to get out of here.

But...

Dad. Dad's face, in her mind's eye again.

Be strong, my love. Be brave. Do the right thing.

She took a deep breath.

Swallowed a lump in her throat.

And then she jumped off the side of the kitchen sink and down onto the floor, right beside Dwayne.

Dwayne looked down at her. He pushed her back. His eyes widened. His mouth moved.

But she didn't hear him. She wasn't listening to him.

She walked around him. Right in front of him. And she stood there. Stood there and remembered how scared she'd felt in the toilet with Mrs Thompson. Thought about how terrified she was. Thought about how she just wanted to make all this go away, and find Dad, and be okay again, for everything to be okay again.

And then she felt something. Hands. Hands, from her side. Grabbing her. Then pushing her back to the sink. Dwayne. Trying to move her. Trying to lift her. Trying to urge her to run away.

But she turned to the bad people.

She turned to them, and she looked at them as they scrambled towards her.

The man in the police uniform stretched out his blood-soaked hands and snapped his cracked teeth.

A woman beside him, pale with long blonde hair, stretched out to grab her with those long fingernails.

And between them, an old man with grey hair, dragging himself across the floor, trying to get to her, crawling towards her like a baby.

She saw them all flying towards her, and she looked at them, shaking, and she took a deep breath.

Be strong.

Be brave.

You've got this, my girl. You've...

And then she felt the long fingernails stick right into both of her arms.

PETE

* * *

The second Helen smiled at him across the room, Pete knew she was planning on doing a runner.

It hurt him. Cut him deep. Like a knife to the back, or a punch to the stomach. Whatever. She wanted out of here. And he could see it etched right across her face.

He looked down at Billy, lying there on the floor. Shit. He was a mess. And Pete still couldn't really accept himself that *he'd* done that. He'd caused that mess. Human life was so damned fragile.

But looking down at him lying there, Pete felt something else. He felt... anger. Pure anger, right in the middle of his chest.

He felt no pity towards this prick at all. Especially not the way he spoke to him.

And if Helen had to suffer a little for the time she'd spent with this bastard, well she had to suffer.

He turned around. Slowly. Back to the patio doors, which he was currently boarding up. He waited a few seconds, his heart racing. 'Cause he knew what Helen was going to try next.

And then he turned around.

Helen was running across the lounge. Over to the door.

And Pete felt it once again like a punch to the stomach. She was leaving him. She was doing a runner. After everything, she was doing a frigging runner.

He felt the sadness, he felt the sense of betrayal, and then he felt something else.

Hatred.

She flew through the lounge door, and he knew he couldn't hold back any longer.

He ran. Ran through the kitchen. Ran towards her. And before she could walk another step, he grabbed her around her ankle, sent her tumbling face flat to the floor.

She let out a yelp. He climbed on top of her. Held her down. "Where do you think you're going?"

"Get the hell off me!" she shouted, punching and slapping and scratching at Pete.

Pete pushed her down even further, grabbing her arms in one large hand. "You need to calm down. You need to stop being hysterical."

"You just killed my fucking partner," Helen shouted. "You need to wake up, Pete. Wake the fuck up."

"*I'm* your partner," Pete said. "It—it was in sickness and in health, remember? We were supposed to conquer everything together. We were supposed to work through problems. Remember?"

"Listen to yourself, Pete. For one moment just listen to yourself."

Pete shook his head. He realised he was crying. Saltiness crept across his lips, and snot filled his throat. For a moment, for just a moment, he saw a flash of himself, as if from above. Pinning down his wife on the floor of their beautiful home. Two dead people in the house with them.

"What are you doing?" he muttered. "What—what are you doing?"

And then he let go of her.

He stepped away from her. Shaking. Because—because this wasn't him. This wasn't right. Today... today had been just so terrifying and so disorienting and so confusing. He wanted to wake up from this nightmare. He wanted to wake up from this bad dream.

"I just don't want to lose you again," Pete sobbed.

Helen got up to her feet. She backed away. She looked right at him, right into his eyes, and he saw that *fear* again. That uncertainty. The same fear and uncertainty he'd seen when he'd thrown the ash tray at her that day. And he hated that look. He hated that expression. It made him feel so ashamed. It made him feel so... afraid.

"You're not leaving," Pete spluttered. Staggering towards her. "I'm—I'm not letting you leave."

And Helen nodded. She nodded, and she took a step towards him. "I know, honey. I—I know. I'm not going anywhere. I'm... I'm staying right here. With you. We can—we can work through this. We can sort it out. Right?"

And hearing these words... they were like honey. Like soft, sweet, tobacco-infused honey. And it almost didn't matter that Pete was highly sceptical of them, or that he suspected that she must be saying them for... for some reasons he was unsure of. Just the fact she was saying those words was beautiful to him.

She stepped up to him. Right up to him. And she looked into his eyes.

"Thank you," Pete said. "Thank—thank you."

She opened her mouth, and moved in towards his ear.

"You always were a pathetic bastard," she said.

And then the next thing Pete knew, before he could process anything... he felt a heavy crack, right across the middle of his head, and everything went blurry as he tumbled down to the floor below.

KEIRA

* * *

Keira looked into Dad's eyes and felt herself on the verge of doing something dangerous. Opening up.

And then she heard the chorus of snarls and gasps, right down the street, right behind her.

She turned around and she saw them right away. Four of those figures. Clearly infected, if indeed that's what this was: an infection. Their arms shook and flailed in inhumane positions. Their necks twisted, turned, and rocked back and forth in a whiplash-inducing manner.

And they were running towards Keira, Dad and the dog, Rufus, with a look that reminded her of kids in a schoolyard—no care for how they looked, no self-consciousness whatsoever.

One of the men was wearing a blue outfit. He looked... he looked like Omar. And when she thought of Omar, her stomach sank. That poor man. And his poor daughter. Out there, somewhere. Most likely at school—if she hadn't already made her way home.

But she couldn't wallow in this sense of sadness for too long.

Because these infected people weren't slowing down.

They were getting closer.

"We need—we need to go," Dad said. And as much as she was sick of running already, as much as she just wanted all this to end, and the police or the military to seize some kind of control and everything to go back to normal... she knew on one hand, that was irrelevant right now. Her wants were irrelevant. Because she was fighting for survival.

And there was another feeling, too. Another sense. A sense that even if things returned to some kind of normality... nothing would ever be "normal" again.

"We need to go, Keira. Now."

And when Keira heard his voice, after that initial reluctance, after that initial determination to do the exact opposite of whatever Dad suggested... Keira knew he was right.

She turned around and she ran.

She ran by Dad's side. She ran, Rufus beside them, panting, wagging his tail, like he was enjoying this; like he was having fun. She saw more smashed car windows. People inside some of them, curled up, hiding. And she ran past one and she saw blood on the windscreen, and she didn't want to look. She didn't want to see it. She didn't want to see *anything*.

She just focused on the road ahead and kept on running.

Up ahead, she saw Omar's street. Hannover Street. Looming in the distance. She was so close. So, so damned close. So close to her goal. So close to finding Omar's daughter. Even though she knew there was a very slim chance she was at home. She was probably at school. At school, terrified, waiting for her dad. And what was that Jean told her? Something about her being... disabled, or something? Some kind of disability. She couldn't remember.

As she ran, panting, almost hyperventilating, she wondered how the hell she was expected to look after this kid. What the hell she was supposed to do when she found the girl.

No. No point thinking about that shit right now. Absolutely no point whatsoever. She had to focus on her own damned survival, first.

She ran. Dad beside her. Rufus between them. Those screaming, growling lunatics closing in on their every step.

And she could see Omar's road in the distance, creeping closer.

Just a few more steps.

Just a few more damned steps...

And then she saw something.

In a car, to her right. A little girl. Lying there. Holding on to her grandma, who lay dead, and covered in blood, right beside her.

And Keira's stomach knotted. She wanted to get into the car. She wanted to save the girl. She wanted to save everyone. And—and that was the problem. She wanted to save everyone... but she couldn't. She just couldn't.

And then she heard a noise, as she ran past, that made her freeze.

A yelp.

A pained yelp.

And then a bark.

She turned around.

Dad crouched on the road, right beside a black Land Rover. He was clutching on to his ankle. Wincing.

"Dad!" Keira shouted.

He looked up at her. Wide-eyed. Rufus stood beside him, kicking back his feet, growling, barking.

And behind them both... those infected people.

Getting closer.

Uncomfortably closer.

She looked over her shoulder. Shit. Hannover Street. Just around the corner. She was so close. And it looked clear up there. If she could make it to Hannover Street, she could make it to

Omar's place. She could hide in there, or around there. Hide from the infected people. Shelter, for as long as she needed to.

But then she turned back around.

Dad looked up at her. Holding his ankle. Wide-eyed. Shaking his head.

"Go," he said. "Just—just go."

And when she heard those words, she felt that familiar pain again. That familiar guilt. The pain of when she'd lost Mum. The guilt over walking away from Dad, severing ties with him, and leading a life of her own.

"Go, Keira," he said. His bloodshot, tearful eyes glistening in the light. "Just... just go."

The infected people hurtled closer.

Closer, and closer.

And Keira's opportunity to escape, her opportunity to get away, it was receding and vanishing by the second.

"Go," Dad shouted. "Go!"

But she took a deep breath.

She shook her head.

She wasn't leaving Dad here on the road to die.

She ran towards him.

His eyes widened, as he crouched there, clutching his ankle. "Keira—"

"Into the car," Keira shouted.

"What? But—"

"The car. Right beside you. Into it. Now. Quick!"

He stood up.

He grabbed the passenger door handle.

And Keira ran around to the driver's side, grabbing the handle.

The infected threw themselves at Dad, as he chucked Rufus into the car, and then tried to climb into the car himself.

They stretched their arms right out towards him.

And then Dad dragged the door open as they gripped his shirt and almost pulled it from his body and—

She flew into the car.

Slammed the door.

And then the infected slammed into the window of the passenger side, as she sat there, panting, shaking, and as Dad sat there in the driver's seat, Rufus on his lap, both looking out at the figures pressed up against the window, scratching the glass with their bloody fingers, and looking in with those dead, pitiful eyes.

And then Dad turned around. Looked right at Keira.

"You should—you should've gone."

"You're welcome," Keira said.

He looked at her, and even though they were surrounded, even though she had no idea how the hell they were getting out of this mess... she smiled back. Maybe it was the adrenaline. Maybe it was the shock. Or maybe it was the goddamned morbidity of everything. But she smiled back.

And then she heard something.

Two things, actually.

Two things that made her skin crawl.

First, a growl. A growl, from Rufus. Who stared right into the back of the car.

And then... as Keira sat there, a shiver creeping up her spine... she heard something else that made her freeze entirely.

Keira heard a gasp.

From the back seats.

They weren't alone.

Someone was in here with them.

DWAYNE

* * *

Dwayne stood at the window and watched the infected surrounding Nisha, and he couldn't actually believe what he was witnessing.

Firstly, Nisha. That kid. That brave young kid, standing right there beside him, refusing to leave his side. And then... and then when he tried to push her back, when he tried to protect her, she pushed his hand away. Stood there. In front of him. Like... like *she* wanted to protect *him*.

Which was... sweet. But it was also terrifying. Because he wanted to get her out of here. He wanted to help her out through that window. And then—and then whatever happened to him, well, it happened. Bloody hell, Dwayne. Why so selfless all of a goddamned sudden?

But the infected. They—they ran towards Nisha. They stretched out their hands towards her. And he pictured all kinds of horrors in his mind's eye. He pictured every manner of awfulness. He saw them landing on her. Ripping her apart.

He stood there and he braced himself when...

Something happened.

The infected. They—they stopped. They grabbed Nisha. They yanked her towards them. And they pulled their snapping, biting mouths towards her, and...

And then they just stopped.

Dwayne stood there. Shaking. He couldn't believe what he was looking at. He couldn't wrap his head around what he was witnessing. These—these people. These enraged, infected people. He'd seen them committing such atrocities. He'd seen them responsible for such horrible things. Ripping chunks out of innocent people. Biting them and them catching it and changing into those aggressive monsters and...

And Nisha was just standing there.

The infected people were all standing around her. Some of them holding her. Some of them just... just sniffing the air. Staring blankly into space. Almost like there was an invisible barrier around Nisha, surrounding her.

And... and he didn't get it. He couldn't believe what he was looking at. He didn't understand. Maybe—maybe time was just moving slowly. Maybe time was just... standing still. Maybe they were all going to launch themselves onto her, wrestle her to the floor.

But they were all standing around her, as she stood in front of him.

As she... *protected* him.

But Dwayne was well aware that his time was ticking. His time was running out.

His luck wasn't going to last forever.

He looked around. At the open window. He could get himself out through there. He could climb out, and he could run across the yard, and then he could get to Mum's care home.

And then when he found her... he could get her out of there.

But then he looked back. Back at Nisha, standing there in

front of him. And then back at the crowd of infected people surrounding her, and therefore surrounding him.

He couldn't run away. Maybe once upon a time, he might've run away. He might've fled.

But that day was not today.

And Nisha was not the person he was going to run from.

So as much danger as he knew he was putting himself in... Dwayne reached down.

He scooped Nisha up.

And then he spun around and he dragged her towards the open window.

Immediately after he grabbed her, the infected people snarled and growled. They all launched at the sink. Slammed against it, one of them grabbing Dwayne's ankle, which he kicked away.

And then he lifted Nisha. He pushed her out of that window. She turned back to him. Wide-eyed.

"Right behind you," he gasped. "Right..."

And then something awful happened.

The window. The window he'd just pushed Nisha through.

It slammed shut.

He stood there. Stood there on the sink. The infected people clambered behind him, all trying to climb to their feet. They'd surrounded him. He was—he was trapped. Nisha was out, but he was trapped. And he was going to die here. He was going to die here for his... for his selflessness. One damned selfless act in his entire frigging life, and it was going to kill him.

He looked around at the infected.

He looked at all their distant eyes.

Their angry faces.

And... and even though he was afraid, there was something about them that made him feel a sense of pity.

Of total pity.

He stood there and he felt this warmth suddenly take over

him. The image of Mum, in his mind's eye. Her own eyes glowing, and her smile glistening, joyful.

"I'm so proud of you, Dwayne. I'm so proud of you, my boy."

He stood there, and he took a deep breath, as the chorus of gasps and growls echoed through the kitchen.

"I wish I could've done more for you," Dwayne said. "I wish I'd been better for you."

He saw the first of the infected clamber onto the side of the kitchen sink, and he knew his time was over.

And then he heard a smash.

A smash, right behind him.

And he felt something hit him. Something heavy. Almost knocked him off the sink and into the ocean of infected people beneath him.

When he looked around, he saw what it was.

Exactly what it was.

Nisha. Standing there. A brick lay beside him. And the glass was broken. She'd smashed it. She'd smashed it open—for him.

He felt fingers against his ankles.

Against his legs.

And at that moment, he knew he had no time to wait around anymore.

No time to waste.

He jumped out of the kitchen window, onto the concrete back yard.

He looked around at the infected, trying to claw their way out of the smashed window.

He took Nisha's hand.

And then, together, they ran across the yard, away from this house, away from the infected, and towards whatever lay ahead.

HELEN

* * *

Helen ran as fast as she could across the field and didn't look back.

But she couldn't escape the memory of what she'd just done.

She kept seeing him. Pete. Holding her down. And then—and then standing up. Looking at her with this completely pitiful expression. She heard the desperation in his voice. She heard him apologising, so pathetically. And she knew she had her moment. She knew she had an opportunity. She knew she had a chance.

So she grabbed the ornament on the mantelpiece and she cracked him over the head.

And then she turned around and ran.

She ran across the field, almost losing her footing. The field was due to be built in, so they'd surrounded it with Harris fencing, but there was an open section she'd managed to run through. The grass was tall though. So tall. So tall that she was confident she could hide in it, if she had to.

But she hoped she wouldn't have to. It was still so close to home. Too close to home.

She didn't want to look back at the cottage. She didn't want to look over her shoulder, to where she lived. To her home. To the home Pete held over her as a power thing, for so long.

Because she didn't even want to think about what she'd done.

She looked down at her hands. Saw blood. Pete's blood? Or was it from Billy? Shit. She didn't know. She wasn't sure. She just —she just didn't know how it was going to look to an outsider. Three bodies. And her, on the run. Shit. Had she killed him? Fuck. Fuck, fuck, fuck. This was a nightmare. She was living in a nightmare, and she wanted to wake up. She wanted to wake up so badly and for this horrible dream to end.

She saw the fencing in the distance. The pathway, just beyond it. She had to get over that fencing. And then she had to go onto the pathway, and then she had to run up that bridleway and she'd reach the farm. John. The farmer. She always chatted to him whenever she was on her morning jog. He always told her that he never liked Pete all that much. Said he was a phoney. And the more people said stuff like that, the more it dawned on her that maybe they were right. And that helped her justify the collapse of the marriage to herself a little more.

But right now she just had to get to John's place. He'd let her in. He'd let her hide there. He'd let her shelter there, until whatever the hell was going on with the angry people settled down, anyway.

She looked over her shoulder, instinctively, even though she was trying her best not to, and she saw movement over by the site entrance.

Shit. He couldn't be... following her, could he? No. Surely not. She'd given Pete a fair hit over the head, a fair crack. There was no way he was on his feet again already.

She turned around. Ran over to the fence at the far end of the field, struggling to stay on her feet. She reached it. Tried to pull the panels apart, because it was a public right of way, and she had every damned right to move them. And besides. She had bigger problems to worry about.

But... the fence.

It wouldn't budge.

Cable ties.

"Shit." Not today. Not today of all days.

She tried to yank the metal fencing away. But it just wouldn't budge. Damn it. She was going to have to climb it. She was going to have to climb it and she was going to have to drop to the other side. She didn't have a damned choice.

She looked back again. Saw movement. Movement in the tall grass, racing through the field. Or... or did she? Did she see that? Or was it just a figment of her imagination? She wasn't sure. She couldn't be sure.

But she knew she needed to get the hell away from here for sure.

She climbed up the fence. Dragged herself to the top. Wished she'd kept herself fitter, wished she'd stuck to swimming, because dragging her bodyweight over that fence wasn't easy—and she wasn't even that heavy.

And when she climbed over it, when she reached the top, she felt the fence wobbling, shaking, and...

She tumbled down to the grass on the other side. Hit the ground with a crash. Her right leg ached like mad. A pain shot right up it. She let out a yelp. Shit. Just her luck to sprain an ankle, or break a bone, or whatever she'd done.

She stood up. Started to run again. Shit. Her leg hurt like mad. But... but it wasn't too bad. It wasn't awful. She could move on it. She was going to be okay.

She climbed over the wobbly stile. And then she stepped onto the bridleway. She loved it down here. Felt like real countryside. Felt like real peace, contrasting the rest of Preston, which seemed to be a free for all for house builders and developers these days.

Other than the bitey horseflies, she had nothing to worry about down here.

Unless the Twitter rumours about bitey people were true. That's how it spread, apparently. Only some people said it was scratches. Some people said it was blood. Others said it was just being in contact with these people for too long. She didn't know. Didn't have a clue.

She ran down the bridleway. Not looking back at the field once. She didn't want to know if Pete was after her. She didn't want to know if he was close. She just... wanted to keep on running. She just wanted to keep on going. She just wanted to get to Farmer John, and then for him to let her in and for everything to be okay, and...

Billy.

She was supposed to be going away with Billy in two weeks. A last-minute trip to Gran Canaria. Beaches. Beer. A good laugh, just the two of them.

She sobbed. Sobbed, as she ran. The reality. The realisation of what'd happened, welling up inside her, at last.

Billy was gone.

Billy was gone, and Pete had killed him.

Billy was gone, Pete had gone crazy, and now she'd... hurt Pete? *Killed* Pete?

She ran down the track and saw the farm up ahead. Saw the cows, shuttered away in their barns. She saw the log store beside her, towering over her, the smell of freshly cut wood even more comforting than usual.

And then she saw the farmhouse, just up ahead.

She took a deep breath. Or as deep a breath as she could manage, anyway. She ran further down the path, closer to the farm. John would be out somewhere. He was always out and about on his farm. Maybe by the little office, beside the calves. He'd be in there. He'd be in there, and she could find him, and she could tell him what'd happened, and he'd look out for her, and he'd protect her until all this blew over, and...

Suddenly, she saw him.

A momentary sense of relief. Farmer John. Standing there. Right in front of her. Looking right into her eyes.

And then she saw what he was holding, what was in his hands, and another feeling crawled through her body.

First, confusion.

Then, fear.

Because Farmer John was holding a shotgun.

"Step back, Helen," he said. "Not another step. Or I'll fire, I tell you. I'll fire."

DAVID

* * *

David heard the groan behind him and all the hairs on his body stood right on end.

The infected banged on the car windows. A gaunt blonde woman scratched the window with her long false nails. An Asian bloke bashed the glass with a tightened fist. And beside him, Rufus barked, and Keira... Keira breathed heavily. She was scared. His girl was scared. Of course she was. Of course she fucking was.

But it was that groan behind him that really captured his attention. And really filled him with fear.

He turned around. Slowly. A part of him didn't want to even see what was on the back seat. Even though his imagination had already done the hard work for him. There was one of these infected people back there. And—and they were going to leap forward and attack him and attack Rufus and attack Keira and...

And then he turned around and he saw her.

It was a woman. About his age probably, maybe a little younger. She... she looked like she was crying. Only it wasn't just tears rolling down her face. It was blood, too. Red tears of blood, leaking right down her face.

She was gasping. Gasping, as more blood oozed out of her lips. And holding onto something, too. Something... something on her arm. Something...

He saw it then.

The blood.

The blood, seeping out of her forearm.

And on the seat beside her, the little boy.

David stared at the little boy and he couldn't believe what he was seeing. The little boy. His brown hair. Lying there on the back seat. Dead. Staring right up at David with those completely dead eyes.

"I had to," the woman gargled. "He wouldn't... he wouldn't stop. He wouldn't stop..."

And suddenly, as David sat there in the driver's seat, surrounded by the infected as they banged away at the car like that polar bear did on the YouTube video he saw just a couple of days ago to try and break inside... the true horror of this situation pieced itself together, right before him.

The boy. The little boy beside the woman had turned into one of these angry monsters. And then he'd bitten his mum. And she'd... she'd killed him. She'd killed him.

"Kill me," she gasped. More blood pouring down from her eyes. Her face turning paler. Blood vessels bursting through her skin, purple and piercing. "Kill me. Kill me now."

And David felt such a wave of sympathy for this woman. She wanted to die. She wanted to die for what she'd done. For what she'd been forced by instinct to do.

But there was nothing he could do for her.

She was going to... she was going to change. Just like everyone else who had been bitten changed.

"There's an opening," Keira said. "We—we might have a way out. Look. See."

And David turned around. He saw a gap. A gap in the infected, enraged people. A gap that led out of the car, onto the street. A chance. A chance to get away. A chance to get out of here. A chance to run.

But David's attention was still on the woman.

He saw her, lying there against the headrest, spluttering blood.

"Kill me," she said. "Kill me. I want—I want to be with him. Please. Please."

And he heard her begging and he felt frozen. He felt like he couldn't move. He felt like...

The tires, screeching across the road.

The scream.

The thump.

David. Please. Please!

And then he was right back here again, as someone grabbed him.

He looked. Keira. Staring at him with wide, tearful eyes.

"It's now or never," she said. "We have to run. We have to go."

He looked back at the woman. Watched, as her eyes grew hazier. As she outstretched her shaking hand, tried to reach him, tried to grab him.

"Please," she said. "Have mercy. Kill... kill me. Please."

And as David sat there, he swallowed a lump in his throat.

"I'm sorry," he said. "I'm... I'm so sorry."

And then he turned around as Keira opened the car door, launched himself out of the car, with Rufus by his side, and ran as fast as his dodgy foot would allow, as a small crowd of infected followed.

And every step he ran, he felt guilt.

Because every step he ran... he heard that woman's desperate cries.

NISHA

* * *

Nisha stood by Dwayne's side and tried to take deep breaths like Dwayne told her to by the nasty man's car earlier. But she couldn't stop shaking.

They ran away from the bad people and climbed over a metal fence into a field with long grass. Dwayne led her through some thick trees towards this weird brick building, which smelled like wee, with pink and yellow pictures of rude things drawn across it. He took his shirt off, and he started looking at the wounds on his body. He had quite a lot. But... but they didn't look like teeth marks. And that's what Nisha was worried about. Teeth marks. They were the wounds she needed to worry about. The wounds *everyone* needed to worry about. Because it was those bites that made people angry, and maybe hungry, and made people do horrible things.

Nisha saw some of the wounds on Dwayne's body. Some of them looked old, like scars. And he had lots of them. Lots of little marks on his back. A patch of skin that looked angry red. And bigger cuts, too.

And she realised she really knew nothing about this man. Maybe he was bad. Maybe he wasn't a good person. He'd helped her, and she'd helped him a bit too... but maybe she'd got him wrong.

He looked at her. Like he didn't realise she was looking at him before. Then he put his shirt on again, which was bloody and split in places. Then he put his jacket back on over it, reached into his pocket, pulled out his notepad and started writing.

You okay?

Nisha nodded. Dwayne nodded back. He didn't say anything to her. He didn't try to mouth words to her that she didn't understand, which was good cause it annoyed her whenever people tried to do that, 'cause she never did understand.

He didn't try speaking. And that... made her feel comfortable, in a weird way. Dad was like that sometimes. She found it tiring signing and trying to understand what other people were signing. So sometimes it was better just to be together. Better just to be quiet. Better just to... to know someone was there.

And it was a while before Dwayne reached for the notepad again. Scribbled onto it.

You saved my life back there. You shouldn't have.

Nisha shrugged. Looked away.

How did you stop them attacking?

Nisha shook her head. Shrugged again. She didn't know what to say. How *had* she stopped them attacking? She hadn't *done* anything. She'd just... stood there. Like she'd stood there when Mrs Thompson attacked her in the toilets.

But even though they hadn't attacked her then, she still found them... scary. And maybe she'd just been lucky. Maybe the next bad people she came across wouldn't leave her. Maybe they'd bite her, and maybe she'd go the way her teachers went, go the way the other kids at school went, go the way Beth went...

She thought of Beth and she felt a lump in her throat.

She hadn't known Beth long. But she missed Beth.

She looked up and saw Dwayne was holding up another page. She expected more questions. More questions about how she'd stopped the bad people. And to be honest she was just tired. She wanted to go home. She wanted to find Dad.

But when she read what was on the page... she realised this was different.

Where are you from? I can take you there.

And it made a knot tighten in her chest. Because she knew what Dad said about trusting strangers. And she'd seen herself already what happened when she trusted strangers. She got into their cars and they turned out to be even worse than Dad described.

But then she saw him writing something else.

And then he turned the page around again.

Don't worry. I'm just trying to find my mum. She's at a care home near here. If your home's near here, I can take you on way.

She felt a knot in her neck. A tightness. And she felt... like she was upset. Like she was going to cry. But it was more that this man had been so nice to her and so helpful to her that she felt really happy he was here, even though she didn't even know who he really was. She felt... grateful. That was the word, wasn't it? The one Mrs Thompson told class they should always be. Grateful.

Hard to feel grateful when you had no hearing and no friends, because you were a different colour to the others, and liked different food, and had a weirder name than the rest of them, and didn't celebrate Christmas.

But right now... Nisha thought she understood what "grateful" was.

She reached for the pad. Wrote a few words, slowly, carefully. Then she held it up to show Dwayne.

Looking for home. Dad. Hannover Street.

Dwayne read the words carefully. Then nodded. Reached for the pad. Wrote more words. Lifted the pad.

I can take you there. Not far.

And seeing those words... once again, Nisha felt this warm feeling in her chest. This overwhelming sense of warmth, deep inside.

She raised her hands, and she signed: *Thank you.* And smiled.

And she could tell from the look on Dwayne's face that he understood. 'Cause then he shook his head, and tried to copy her. *Thank you.*

He smiled at her. And she smiled back at him. And even though she was covered in blood, and could smell metal, and felt so sick and so scared... right now, Nisha felt something she hadn't felt all day.

Right here, with Dwayne, Nisha felt safe.

PETE

* * *

Pete opened his eyes and wondered if this entire morning had been some kind of godawful dream.

And then he tasted blood.

His vision was all blurry. He could see something right in front of him. Something... something like wood. Dark wood. And... and was that *blood* he could see?

He was dreaming. He was still half-asleep. 'Cause the shit he'd seen... that shit couldn't be real. It had to be a figment of his imagination. Watching Stan get his throat torn away by Colin. Leaving that boy alone in the police car. Coming back to Helen's, and knocking her new piece Billy down to the floor, and then her trying to run away, and...

A crack.

A heavy crack. Right across his head.

A sickening tightness clutched his chest. The dream. The dream that felt so, so real.

His heart thumped. The taste of blood in his mouth grew stronger. And there was a haziness to his vision. The smell of wood. The taste of sweat. And... and the solid floor, right beneath him.

He pushed himself up. Looked around. He was in his lounge. The lounge of his and Helen's cottage.

Only...

He looked down. Saw blood on the floor, right beneath him. And then saw a drop of blood, trickling down onto the wood. Blood. Blood coming from *his* head. Something had happened to him. Someone had *attacked* him.

He looked up again. Saw that prick Billy lying there, nothing recognisable left of his mashed-up face. And then across the kitchen, he saw the partly boarded up patio doors, which he had been working on so recently.

He saw it all, and then he remembered pinning Helen down, telling her she was going to be okay, that he was sorry, as he climbed off her, begging her, pleading her to give him a second chance, for her to let him make amends for the sins of the past, and...

And she'd walked towards him. She'd walked towards him and told him yes, she was going to give him a second chance, she was going to stay here, and they were going to be okay, everything was going to be okay, and...

And then that crack.

Right across his head.

And then waking up on the floor. The taste of blood between his teeth.

He stood there, ears ringing, head spinning, and he wanted to cry. She'd—she'd hit him. She'd hit him and then she'd... she'd done a runner. Out through the front. She'd done a runner and she'd left him for *dead* on the floor.

And he felt tears welling up in his eyes. Because—because that was evil. That was cruel. That was so, so cruel. After everything he'd done for her. After all the sacrifices he'd made for her. *That* was how she treated him?

And then he felt his sadness transforming. He felt it morphing. He felt it taking on a new form entirely. A new form he recognised well. Very well.

He felt that sadness turning into anger.

He took a deep, shaky breath.

And then he tightened his fists, cracking his knuckles.

He looked out the window, out at the fields beyond *his* lovely cottage.

He was going to find her.

And he was going to make her regret ever taking advantage of his better nature.

KEIRA

* * *

Keira looked over her shoulder and when she finally saw they weren't being chased, she collapsed to her knees in a moment of sheer exhaustion.

It was cloudy above. Boiling hot. Sweat poured down her forehead, and onto her face. But she couldn't stop shaking, either. A sickening nausea clawed through her body, climbing its way right up from her stomach and into her throat, tightening and tightening every second...

She felt a warm hand on her shoulder. Flinched. Looked around. Dad stood there, staring down at her, wide-eyed. He wasn't saying anything. Wasn't saying anything at all. But for that moment, for that one moment where she forgot what happened between them, forgot the distance between them, and forgot what happened to *Mum*, too... for that one moment, she felt comforted by his presence.

She took a deep breath. In through her nose. Then puffed her lips out. The air constantly stunk of smoke. She could still hear screaming filling the streets. Sirens in the distance, although fewer now. Above, helicopters flew over. Military, by the looks of things. A beacon of hope amidst the chaos. But also... also, somewhat worrying. Because the presence of the military really drove home the severity of the situation. As severe as Keira already realised it was.

And then she stood up. And stood tall at that. Took another deep breath, and focused on the task at hand. She was on Hannover Street now. Which meant she was on Omar's road. She could get to his house. With any luck, his daughter might be here. And if not... she could at least locate her school. The thought of the journey stretching ahead was exhausting. She just wanted to sleep. Shit. She was on a night shift last night too, wasn't she? She'd forgotten. She was absolutely knackered. Absolutely exhausted. She wanted to sleep for an eternity. But at the same time, she wasn't sure the adrenaline was going to let her.

"We're on the street," Dad said. "The one you were looking for."

Keira heard his voice and for a moment, another knot tightened in her stomach. His voice sounded so shaky. The incident. The incident in the car. The woman. Begging... begging him to kill her. And having to run away, through that crowd of oncoming infected. That shit was rough. Especially after what happened, all those years ago.

She looked around at Dad. Half-smiled. Nodded. "Thank you."

Dad shrugged. "What for?"

"I've... I've been hard on you today."

"Keira, we've been through a lot. You've been through—"

"You have to understand this... this isn't always so easy. For me to process. You... you being here right now. And if I snap, it's not because I'm not grateful that you're here. I am. Really. But I just..."

She didn't say another word. And glancing up into Dad's eyes, she knew she didn't have to. He got it. And as critical as she was of him, as much as a part of her really didn't want him here right now... that was something she couldn't hold against him.

"The car," Keira said. "What happened back there. With the woman. You couldn't... you couldn't have done anything more—"

"I could've done more," Dad said.

Keira shook her head. "She... she was already gone. You couldn't have helped her. You couldn't have—"

"If I'd not frozen, I could've... I could've got to her. I could've saved her. I could've saved... I could've saved both of them."

And when he looked at Keira, she realised he wasn't talking about the woman from the car earlier today. Not anymore. He was talking about Mum. He was talking about the past.

Heat built up in her face. She tried to gulp, but she couldn't. She tried to breathe deeply, but that wasn't easy either.

She turned away. Looked across the street, over at Omar's place, right there in the distance. And she knew they needed to get off this street. The momentary respite they'd enjoyed for the last however many minutes was rare. And those moments of respite were going to become even rarer as the day went on. That's what it felt like, anyway.

"Come on," Keira said. "We should... we should search Omar's place. Before—"

"I am sorry, Keira," Dad said. His voice all shaky. "And I... I understand. Why you stopped... why you stopped looking me in the eye. Why you stopped visiting me. I understand."

She looked around at him and she saw this spectre of a man. A ghost of his former self.

She looked right into his wide eyes, swallowed a lump in her throat, and nodded.

"Come on," she said. Falling just short of saying "I forgive you," the words she knew he craved to be put out of this eternal misery. "Let's go search Omar's place."

And then she turned around, and with Rufus trailing right

behind her, she walked through the chaos, towards Omar's, and towards whatever unpredictable horrors awaited.

DWAYNE

* * *

Dwayne walked by Nisha's side on the way to Mum's care home and wondered what in the name of hell he was doing.

It was cloudy now. He had no idea what time it was. He didn't wear a watch, and his phone battery had died. Typical. Fucking typical. But it felt like afternoon. Which was mental. Deep down, it felt like an eternity had passed since he was sitting in Nico's hire car, caught up in traffic on the motorway. And even longer since the hours *before* the robbery. Shit. Was this his punishment for messing around with karma one too many times?

He walked through the tall grass of a bunch of fields behind the main hustle and bustle of the suburbs. They were due to start building here soon, which meant they'd erected a bunch of fences, designed to keep people out. But the way Dwayne saw it, it gave him a decent level of protection from the nutters running rampant through the city. Not perfect, sure. Anyone could break through a bit of Harris fencing.

But it was better than being on the streets.

And yet... he had a problem.

He looked down. Saw the kid, Nisha, walking beside him. And just looking at her made a whole bunch of questions race through his head. What the hell was he doing? He couldn't look after a kid. He could barely even look after his damned self.

And besides. He didn't *want* to care for anyone but himself. Except for Mum. What was he doing getting caught up in a kid's dramas? So he'd helped her. Sure, he'd helped her. But he could've left her miles back. Left her somewhere safe. Told her to lay low until all this settled. But maybe partly because he was beginning to doubt this *would* settle, and also because of some sense of deep responsibility he felt for this kid... he wasn't too keen on the idea of just leaving her somewhere.

And then there was the fact that she'd saved him.

Standing there. In front of those infected nuts. Standing there and watching as some kind of barrier formed in front of her. Protecting herself. And protecting *him* somehow, too.

He didn't understand it. He didn't know what the hell was going on. But if this *was* some kind of mass pandemic, then the fact that the infected didn't seem to be going for the kid might come in handy—not just for himself, but for others, too.

But there was more to it than that. He'd only known the girl for a matter of hours. And "known" was a bit of an exaggeration. The girl couldn't speak. Or didn't seem to want to, anyway. She was deaf, and spoke via written word and occasionally sign language that he didn't understand, apart from *Thank you* now.

But... yeah. It wasn't just for selfish reasons he wanted this kid around. A part of him wanted to look after her. Protect her. She'd been through hell. And she seemed like a good kid.

He turned around and he looked back at the houses in the distance. Hannover Street wasn't too far away. He could stop by there, check on her dad, and then carry on towards his mum's care home. But what was he going to do with the girl when he took her home? Leave her there? That would be the logical thing to do, right?

But... no. No, he wasn't sure. Nothing seemed logical. Nothing seemed *right*.

But then again, he needed to focus on getting her there in the first place.

He felt a nudge on his left hand. Looked down. Keira tugged his finger. He didn't know what she was pointing to, but she was nodding ahead, off into the distance. Her eyes were wide. Scared? Had she seen someone? One of those infected lunatics? Maybe they weren't so safe here after all. They were only a bit of fencing away from being in the suburbs, so probably not.

He looked around. Squinted. And then he saw what she was pointing to.

A deer. A deer, right in the middle of this fencing. Standing there. Looking right over at Dwayne, and at Nisha. Shaking.

And it made Dwayne feel so sad. Seeing it standing here, in the middle of a construction site. Unable to escape the boundaries of the fencing. But also protected from the outside to a degree, too. Just like them.

He was about to keep walking when he saw another deer emerge from behind it.

A smaller deer. By its mother's side. Peering over at him and Nisha. Watching, closely.

And looking at those two deer, mother so protective of her child, he thought about Mum and he felt a wave of guilt. Because he was delaying getting to her. He was delaying getting to her to help this kid he barely knew. And that didn't seem right. It didn't seem fair. It didn't seem...

You're doing the right thing, Dwayne. You're a good boy, and you're doing the right thing.

And then Brighton.

The screams.

The heat.

The smoke.

"Please!"

And then he shook his head and he saw the deer run off, across the site.

He stood there, the smoke still fresh in his nostrils, and very much real, very much not a figment of his imagination. He took another deep breath. Looked down at Nisha. Nodded.

It was time to get her back to her home.

And then it was time to go find Mum.

And there was no more time for delaying. He was going to find Mum, and he was going to save her.

No matter what it took.

HELEN

* * *

"Back away, Helen. Turn right the hell around and back away. Right now."

Helen stood there in the middle of the farmyard. Farmer John stood opposite her, holding a shotgun, pointing it right at her. His eyes bulged wide and angry. And that gun shook in his hands, as he gripped it tight and pointed it at her. Seeing him like this, seeing a man she thought was so friendly, so welcoming, so salt of the earth... seeing him on the brink of such violence was so disorienting. And it was a sure sign that something serious was going down. Something very serious.

She held her hands up in the air. Her heart raced. A sickly sensation stormed through her stomach, making her shake even more. "Please, John. I—"

"I don't care what you have to say. I don't care about anything right now. I just... I just want you to get out of my farm. Right this second."

"It's—it's Pete," Helen said. "He's—"

"I don't give a shit about Pete!" John shouted. Waving that

shotgun closer towards her. Cows mooed from the barns beside her. Chickens clucked too. Even they were sounding nervous.

She stood there, and her head spun. Ringing filled her ears. She just wanted to get away from Pete. She just needed... she just needed some *help*.

She looked over her shoulder. Down the bridlepath. Branches swayed in the wind. In the distance, she swore she saw... movement.

"There's something wrong," Helen said, turning back around to John. "With Pete. There's—there's something wrong. And Billy. He—he's... he's... John you need to help me. Billy needs help. He—"

A blast exploded at Helen's feet.

She jolted back. Almost fell over.

John stood there. Pointing the shotgun at her feet. Smoke billowed from the end of it. There was a crater in the ground in front of her. A hole.

She looked up.

John stared right at her. Shaking his head.

"If it wasn't already clear," he said, "I'm serious. Get away. Get away from my farm. Right *now*."

Helen's stomach sank even more. Her heart raced faster. Tingling crept down her fingers, and that tension intensified in her chest.

John might've been friendly in the past. She might've got along great with him in the past. But John wasn't friendly now. John was serious. If she didn't do what he said, John was going to... to *shoot* her? To *kill* her?

What the hell had happened to the men of this world in the last few hours?

Helen looked into John's eyes and she saw tears rolling down his cheeks. She saw this look on his face. This begging look. This look of... this look of resistance. He didn't want to do this. He didn't want to shoot. But he was doing what he felt he had to do. For his family.

And then Helen caught a glimpse of herself. The blood. The blood, all over her hands. And splattered across her chest. And when she looked up and saw the fear in John's eyes... she understood now. This time, she understood.

He thought she was one of... one of these biters she'd heard about. Just like the man who threw himself through her patio window. He thought she was possessed by that same affliction.

"I'm not—I'm not one of them," Helen said.

John lifted the shotgun. Pointed it further towards Helen. His hands weren't shaking quite as much anymore. He looked more focused. He looked more determined. He looked more... assured.

"I know you're a good man," Helen said. "And right now... right now I'm just asking for some help. I just—I just need somewhere to lay low. I just need somewhere to hide. Until... until I lose Pete. And the second all this blows over, the second he's— he's behind bars for what he's done... I don't know how I'll ever repay you but I will. I will."

John shook his head. He puffed out his lips. And he lowered that shotgun, just a little.

"Don't you get it?" he said. "Things ain't ever going back to normal, Helen. The things I've seen. The—the things I've watched on the TV. And the things I've seen in my house. Things ain't ever going back to normal. Ever again."

She looked into his eyes, saw that fear, and heard that fear in his voice, too.

And then she saw something.

His right arm.

Something that sent a shiver, right down her spine.

Tooth marks.

Just like the man who'd flown through their patio.

And just like the reports she'd read about on Twitter. People biting people. Turning... turning aggressive. Turning into these aggressive thugs.

She looked at the tooth marks on his shaking arm. And then she looked up, into his eyes. He looked at her with this look of *knowing* now. Like he knew she'd seen what she'd seen, and there was no hiding from it. Not anymore.

"She just—she just bit me," he said. "Carla. She just... she just said she felt sick, went for a lie down. And then... and then she came in and she bit me."

Carla. John's wife. She'd been on a hen do in the Lakes earlier in the week. Hadn't felt right since she returned. Ended up in hospital for a day, and came home yesterday, and...

"She's just sick," John said. Shaking. Whimpering. "She's—she's just sick. And she needs looking after. The kids. The kids need looking after. They need a father. They need their dad. They need..."

And then she turned around and she saw something.

The curtains.

The curtains at the front of John and Carla's beautiful house.

Twitching.

And a hand.

A woman's hand, scratching right against the glass.

And then... and then two smaller hands.

Two *children's* hands.

A boy.

A girl.

Their kids.

She stared in through the window as Carla appeared. Her eyes looked glassy, dead. Blood covered her chin, and dripped down her neck. And by her side, Sean, their son. An unmistakable bite mark, right across his pale forehead.

And then Saoirse.

That same dead look in her eyes.

Scratching the glass.

Then banging the glass.

Covered in blood.

Helen felt the tears welling up in her eyes. She looked around at John, a crippling pain squeezing the middle of her chest.

"Please," John said. "They just need a father. They just—they just need a dad."

She looked into his eyes, and she shook her head. "I'm sorry," she said. "I'm so... I'm so sorry."

He lowered his shotgun. Cried, as blood seeped from the bite marks on his arm. "I just want to look after them. I just want to protect them. I just... I just want to care for them."

And even though she was terrified, even though she was scared, and even though she was worried that John might imminently go the same way as his wife, and the same way as his kids... she walked up to him, opened up her arms, and felt him fall into hers.

"I'm sorry," she said, as she held him tight, tears streaming down her cheeks, listening to his sobs. "I'm so sorry."

She held John tight as he cried, and in the corner of her eye, she saw his beloved family, all standing at the window, all banging their fists against it, all trying to get out...

"I just wanted to protect them," John whimpered...

DAVID

* * *

David and Keira stood outside this "Omar's" place and David really wanted to get the hell away from here —fast.

He could hear shouting up the road, in the distance. Sirens were a constant companion, only he felt like he was hearing less of them now, as the day progressed. Which... didn't feel like a good sign. The streets were in disarray. If anything, there should be *more* sirens than ever right now. But David couldn't shake the feeling that things were falling apart, and they were falling apart fast.

"This is the place," Keira said.

David turned around. It wasn't much to sing about. A standard small semi-detached house, on quite a quiet street. The garden was overgrown. Weeds covered the cracked flags on the driveway. The windows looked misty, steamy, dusty. It didn't look like anyone was home. But then again, it hardly looked like the sort of place that *ever* looked like anyone was home.

He glanced next door. A perfectly kept garden. Freshly

painted door. New double- glazed windows. Damn. He could tell that whoever lived there must be pissed with this Omar fella, "bringing down" the pair of houses.

He took a deep breath of the smoky air, and he sighed. "Come on. The sooner we've checked this place out, the better."

Keira nodded. And then she walked over to the door. Tried the handle, which inevitably didn't budge.

"Locked," Keira said.

"Yeah," David said. "I could've guessed that much. We live in the twenty-first century, in case you hadn't noticed."

"Fuck off."

She turned around and peeked through the window, but she clearly couldn't see a thing in there. David looked down at Rufus. Rufus looked up at him, wagging his tail. David smiled at him, and Rufus wagged his tail even more. He kind of liked him.

"No spare keys by the door. Shit."

"Yeah," David said. "Not ideal."

"We could try the back."

David looked up. Down the street. Flickers of movement in the distance. Curtains twitching. It seemed... quiet. Too quiet.

"Well whatever we do, I'd appreciate it if we hurried."

He turned around and saw Keira was already halfway down the side of the house. Running down the pathway, towards the back garden.

"Be careful," David said. "Or whatever. Do whatever you want. You will do anyway."

He looked over his shoulder again. Down the street. Saw more movement. Heard more distant screaming.

And then he ran down the path at the side of the house, with Keira.

He reached the back garden. The grass was overgrown. There were weeds everywhere. An old pink castle sat at the bottom of the garden, but it'd fallen victim to moss and mould. The fence was covered in patches and cracks on this side, which the neighbours next door looked like they'd tried patching up.

"And I'm guessing you're going to try the same trick here? Only I'd bet good money these doors are locked too, surprise surprise."

She turned the handle. Sighed. "It would appear so."

A scream echoed down the street. And then a loud, gasping groan. It sounded close. And like it was getting even closer.

"Keira," David said. "I appreciate why you need to be here. And I fully respect what you're trying to do. But... but I'm really not comfortable with this. I'm..."

A smash.

A smash made David spin around, turn right towards Keira. Was she okay? Oh God was she okay?

He turned around.

Keira was standing in front of the patio windows. Only the patio windows weren't intact anymore. They were broken. Smashed.

She turned around. Raised her eyebrows.

"And you think this girl's really gonna appreciate this, is she?"

"She might do," she said. "I made a promise to her dad. I made a promise to a friend. I'd do anything I could to find her. To make sure she's safe. And that's what I intend to do."

And then she walked inside, through the broken glass, into the darkness.

He looked down at Rufus again. Shook his head. "Yeah," he said. "She's pretty much always like this."

He followed her, then. Followed her into the dark house. It smelled musty in here, and damp. In fact, there were damp patches all over the ceiling. Chunks, actual *chunks* of mould, congregating in the corner. Flies buzzed around the unwashed stack of pots. The fruit bowl overflowed with a bunch of blackened bananas, a sickly-sweet aroma lingering in the air.

And then Keira started searching the house. Room by room.

Downstairs. Then charging upstairs, with reckless abandon. Then right back downstairs again.

"No sign," Keira said.

David brushed his fingers through his hair. "As expected."

Keira sighed. "We need... we need to find out what school she goes to." She marched around the kitchen, opening every drawer. "There must be a letter around here. Or a report. There... there must be something."

And as Keira searched the kitchen, David headed upstairs. Omar's room was completely lacking in personality. No pictures on the walls, just nails. Wallpaper, peeling away. A dirty, smelly duvet cover lay on the floor in a heap, while stained underwear covered the off-white bedsheets.

There were no wardrobes in here. No drawers in here. No letters. No letters at all.

He walked out of Omar's room. Walked over towards the next room. Pushed the door, gently.

When he opened the door, he saw Keira's room. It was... old-fashioned. Old carpet that looked like it was from the seventies. Flowery wallpaper, covered in vibrant colours—pinks, and greens, and blues. And books. Lots and lots of books, stacked right around the room. So much more orderly than her father's room. So much tidier than her father's room.

And in the corner of the room... David saw something that caught his eye.

A picture. A little picture. A young girl, Asian. Wearing hearing aids. Wide smile across her face. By her side, a man. Grinning just as widely, with this beaming smile, these kind eyes.

He held the photo in his hands, and he saw a flash of him and Keira in this photo, and then he thought about what Keira said. How this man had died. How this girl had lost her father.

Wherever this kid was... he hoped she was okay.

He hoped *every* displaced kid was okay.

Suddenly, he heard something. On the street. Screaming.

Piercing screaming. He glanced out beyond the net curtains, out through the dirty window at the street below.

Two men. Pinning another man down. Punching him. Beating the shit out of him. Biting at his legs, and at his back, while the poor man on the road cried out in agony. "Help! Help!"

He looked down on the street. Butterflies fluttered inside. They needed to get away from here. They weren't safe here. They needed to get away from this house, and they needed to get away fast.

Because...

Because in the distance, he saw more figures. More of them, at the top of the road. Three more. All of them moving in this possessed, contorted way that told him everything he needed to know about them—about their current state.

He turned around and went to run downstairs for Keira when he saw something dangling by the door.

A bag. A little rectangular navy bag.

And on that bag...

Hollins Primary School.

He grabbed that bag. Heart racing. A flicker of hope glowing inside him. He had it. They had their location. Now—now they could get out of here. Now they could go find that school. Now, they could go find this girl, and they could get out of here, and...

He was about to run out of the room with the bag under his arm when he heard something downstairs that filled him with total, crippling terror.

Downstairs, David heard a scream.

A familiar scream.

Keira's scream.

NISHA

*   *   *

Nisha stood at the fence at the end of her street and even though she was scared, she smiled.

She looked down the road, past the fence that they were building the new houses behind, and she saw her house, right down the road. Her road looked... quiet. There were none of the bad people. There was nobody about at all, actually. Which... was a good thing, wasn't it? Maybe the bad people hadn't made it here. Maybe it was still safe here. Maybe home was going to be okay. Maybe *everything* was going to be okay.

She swallowed a big lump in her throat. Her chest felt sore, like when she'd had an infection when she was younger, and she couldn't stop coughing all night. Everything looked weird. Fuzzy, in a way. And everything *felt* weird, too. She wanted to sleep. She wanted to get home and close her bedroom door and sleep. No— no, she wanted to sleep in Dad's bed, with his warmth beside her. She'd be safe there. She'd be okay there. Everything would be okay by Dad's side.

She took a step towards the fence and suddenly felt a weight stopping her.

She looked down. Dwayne. It was his hand. Holding her. Stopping her from moving. Why was he stopping her? Why didn't he want her to move?

She looked up. He was covering his mouth with a finger. Quiet. He wanted... he wanted her to be quiet.

She looked around and right away, she realised why.

A man. Running down the road. His mouth moving, like he was... like he was screaming. Running as fast as he could. Looking over his shoulder at someone chasing after him.

Her heart started to thud. She felt dizzy. A little bit sick. She'd seen so many bad things. So much... so much blood. So much death. She didn't want to see any more. Especially not on her street. Not outside her home. Where she was supposed to be safe.

She watched this man running past. Dwayne kept his hand against her chest, stopping her from moving. And he kept his finger over his lips, too. She waited. Waited, as he ran down the road. As he staggered forward. As...

Two more people. Running around the corner. Chasing him.

And the way they moved, the way they flailed their arms around, the way their legs twitched from side to side... they were the bad people.

They ran after the man. Kept on chasing him. And Nisha hoped they kept on running. She hoped the man got away. And she also hoped that all of them got off this street, and away from her home.

She stood there, very still. Her home so near, and yet so far away.

And then she saw something awful.

The man tumbled over. Slammed against the road. Within a few seconds, the people chasing him were on top of him, and biting him, and punching him, and blood was splattering everywhere, and...

Dwayne tapped her. On her shoulder. He pointed ahead. And then he moved his hand across his neck, and shook his head.

She knew what he was saying right away. They weren't going down that road. They weren't going anywhere near Nisha's house.

And... and Nisha turned around and she got it. Nisha turned around and she understood. Because—because the blood. The man, on the road. And then... and then him trying to hit back as blood splattered everywhere, and...

Dwayne shook his head again. One hand to her chest. A hand movement, across his neck. And then the finger to his lips again.

A warmth filled Nisha's face. Because—because she couldn't *not* go down this street, because this street was *her* street, and her home was down here. And this was everything she'd been working towards. This was... this was where she'd been trying to get to for forever now.

She turned back to the street. Back to the man. Twitching now. She could make it. She could make it to her house. She could make it to her house and make it through the front door and...

And then another three figures appeared, around the corner.

All of them ran around that bend.

All of them ran towards that screaming man, pinned down on the road.

And Nisha felt cold. Her body wouldn't stop shaking. Her heart wouldn't stop racing. If more of them were coming, then it meant it was even harder for her to get home.

Dwayne suddenly let go of her. He reached into his pocket. Scribbled on the notepad really fast.

And then he held it out to her, almost dropping it.

I'm sorry. Not safe.

But Nisha shook her head. She felt... she felt like she'd been punched in the tummy. Her eyes started stinging. She... she couldn't give up now. She was so close to home. She couldn't just give up.

She shook her head. Looked right up at him, then shook her

head. And then... and then even though she knew he didn't understand, she tried to sign. She tried, and hoped he'd understand.

Maybe I'm safe.

But he just looked at her. He just shook his head. He put his hand to his neck again, and shook it again. Then pointed at the notepad. He looked worried. He looked scared.

She turned around. Saw the three people reach the man in the middle of the road. And then—and then one of them ran off to a house across the road, where the old woman who smelled like fish lived. She didn't know her name, but she hoped she was okay. She really hoped she was okay.

She looked at the four people surrounding that one man on the road. She couldn't see properly, 'cause her eyes were all blurred and stinging.

And then... and then she saw her house. Her house, on the left. So close.

And then... something blocked her vision. A notepad. Right in front of her.

I'm sorry. Nothing we can do.

She took a deep breath. Gulped. Looked around at him.

I'm sorry, he mouthed.

And as she stood there, she closed her burning eyes. And then she took another deep breath, and she nodded.

And then Dwayne tilted his head over his shoulder. *Come on.* That's what he was saying.

She waited for him to turn around, for him to move just a little, when she took a deep breath.

When she turned around.

And even though her chest was tight, and even though her heart wouldn't stop racing... she saw her home, and she saw those people, and then in her mind she saw Dad, at home, waiting for her, so happy, so proud.

And then she saw Mrs Thompson, in the toilets. Holding her. Then letting her go.

And then the crowd in that kitchen, where she'd escaped, with Dwayne.

She might be scared. But what if they *couldn't* hurt her?

And she might be scared.

But she wasn't giving up on getting home. She wasn't giving up on finding Dad.

She took another deep breath, and even though she was crying, and even though she felt like she was going to wet herself, Nisha did the only thing that she felt like she could do right now.

She took another deep breath.

Then she stepped around the fence.

Onto her street.

And then she ran as fast as she could.

PETE

* * *

Pete saw Helen the moment he stepped out of the field, and looked down the bridleway towards the farm.

She was... she was holding someone. Someone... someone had their arms wrapped around her, in the middle of that farmyard. And he couldn't quite understand. Who? Who was holding her? What was happening to her?

And despite his anger, despite the pain splitting through the middle of his head, he felt... worried. What if—what if she was under attack? What if this was one of those infected pricks? What if they'd captured her, and they were biting her, just like Colin bit Stan?

A momentary twinge of satisfaction.

No. Don't think like that. That's not good. That's not right. She's—she's still your wife, at heart. She loves you, deep down. And you love her.

He needed to help her.

So he ran. He ran down the bridleway. A route he always used to run, when he lived this way. He used to love it down here. He loved going off for runs and walks down here, sometimes with Helen, sometimes alone. Even though it wasn't all that far away from civilisation—you could hear the nearby hum of the motorway—it still felt like a secluded paradise away from home.

He still came down here, sometimes. After work. Or even when he was on a quiet shift. He used to pull up, walk down here, then walk across the field. Stare in through the open curtains of Helen's front window. Watch that bastard wrap his arm around her, kiss her, in *his* house.

At least that bastard was dead now. At least that bastard was...

Dead.

Fuck.

He'd—he'd killed him. He'd killed someone. He'd killed someone and—and now he was running after Helen, running after the woman he loved.

He couldn't breathe.

He couldn't think.

He'd killed someone, and he was going to rot in prison, and the other prisoners were going to kick the shit out of him and rape him and throw scalding sugar water over his cock and—

No.

No, he wasn't going to prison. He'd made a deal with himself a long, long time ago. Hypothetically, he always told himself that if ever he were faced with the prospect of prison, he'd kill himself before he had the chance.

And right now?

Right now, he kind of wanted to take Helen with him. Because it wasn't fair that she got to stay alive, that she got to carry on, after everything she'd taken away from him.

But still, he saw her. Right there in that embrace. Still, he saw her, in the arms of that man. Still, he saw her standing there in that farmyard. And he wanted to reach her. He wanted to help her. He wanted to...

And then it hit him like a punch to the gut.

This man. It wasn't just any man. And... and the closer he got, the more he realised he wasn't *attacking* Helen, either.

It was John. The farmer. He never liked that prick. When he and Helen were together, he'd always make sexist remarks, and make her giggle a bit too much, and he'd catch him looking at her arse when she walked past from time to time, too. He was convinced there was something between them. And it made him jealous. So much so that one night, when he was on shifts, he didn't go to work at all. He walked into the field and watched Helen go on her nightly walk, across the field, onto the bridleway, towards the farm...

And then she walked right past the farm. Didn't even turn to look at it.

But—but Pete was convinced there was something going on. He was almost certain there was something there. Maybe she'd seen Pete. Suspected he was following her. Maybe she was on to him, and he'd just timed it badly. He wasn't sure. He didn't have a clue.

But he would never shake that crippling suspicion that something was going on between them.

And now... seeing them holding each other, seeing her hugging him, and seeing his arms around her... it confirmed it all. Confirmed all his suspicions. All his goddamned suspicions. So this was who she ran to when shit hit the fan?

Well, he was going to make sure John knew damned well not to mess with him again—or mess with *his* wife again.

He ran towards them when he saw John look up. His eyes widened. He stepped away. He muttered a few inaudible words under his breath. Then Helen turned around, and that same pattern followed—that same widening of her eyes. That look, like she'd been caught red-handed.

"Well," Pete said, panting. A warm liquid trickled down his head, and when he wiped it away, he realised it was blood. "Looks like you two are nice and cosy here."

"Pete," Helen said. "John. He's... His family—"

"I don't give a shit about John," Pete said, taking a step towards the pair of them. "And I don't give a shit about his family. You come back with me. Right fucking now." And then he looked at John. "And I'll deal with you later."

John shook his head. He stared at Pete with these wide, tearful eyes. And Pete didn't understand. What was happening here? What the hell was happening? Why was he crying? Why was he so sad? Why was he...

And then he saw it.

Blood, dripping from John's arm.

And... were those tooth marks?

"Oh," Pete said.

"My family," John muttered. "I just—I just wanted to look after them. I just wanted to protect them. I just wanted to..."

And then Pete heard something horrifying.

Something that sent a shiver, right up his spine.

Glass, smashing.

An animalistic wail.

And then he looked to his left, over towards the farm house and saw Pete's wife, Carla, and their two kids whose names he couldn't be arsed remembering, clambering out through the living room window and racing towards him.

Screaming.

KEIRA

* * *

Keira rushed around Omar's kitchen and desperately tried to find a single damned sign that pointed her towards Nisha's school.

She yanked the kitchen drawers open. Saw cutlery in one, various pots and pans in another. Shit. How hard could it be to find out which frigging school she went to? It couldn't be that difficult.

And truth be told, wasn't it just a process of elimination, really? Maybe if she headed to the nearest primary school, that would be enough. That would do the trick. Or was that too obvious? She didn't know. She didn't have a clue.

She just had to keep on searching.

She yanked a lower cupboard open. Cereal boxes. Tons of cereal boxes. Coco Pops. Sugar Puffs. Hell, that box of Sugar Puffs looked old. Did they even make Sugar Puffs anymore? And why was she even *thinking* about Sugar Puffs? There were more important matters at hand. Far more important matters at hand.

A shriek echoed down the street. Shivers crept down Keira's spine. That scream. Someone was out there, on the road. Suffering. Another victim to these... to these *infected* people, whoever the hell they were, whatever the hell was wrong with them. They were out there. They were out there on the street, and if Keira wasn't careful, if she wasn't quick, they'd be in here, and they'd be all over her.

She thought about Jean. The tears rolling down her face. The blood, splattering from her body.

She thought about Omar. The way he clutched her hand, and stared up at her with those wide, bloodshot eyes. The way he begged her to protect his daughter. And the way Jean asked the same of her.

She remembered that promise she'd made. A promise she intended to keep.

And then she took a deep breath and resumed her search.

She opened more drawers. She searched more cupboards. But —but there was nothing. There were no signs of Nisha's school. There were no letters, there were no school reports, there was... nothing.

She just needed a sign. One little sign.

She just needed...

The washing machine.

A spark flickered inside her chest. A twinge, ticking her from inside.

The washing machine.

What if...

She ran over to that washing machine door. Swung it open. Saw a stack of washing in there. It smelled damp, like those clothes had been stuffed in there for a long time.

Another scream echoed down the street. Footsteps slammed against the concrete. They sounded closer. They all sounded closer. And getting closer by the second.

She dragged the clothes out of the washing machine, tossing

them all over the kitchen floor. If this didn't work... if this didn't work, she was wasting time. Wasting valuable time.

But if this worked...

If she found what she was looking for...

She dragged more clothes out of the washing machine. Threw more of them across the floor. Her heart raced. Come on. This had to work. Give me something. Lord give me *something*...

And then she saw it.

Right at the back of the washing machine. Sitting there, in a crumpled heap, she saw it.

A jumper.

A blue school jumper.

And a logo etched on it.

A logo she recognised.

Hollins Primary School.

Yes. Hollins. She—she knew where that was. She could get out of here and she could find it. She could get out of here and she could get there and then she could find Nisha. It was going to be okay. Everything was going to be okay.

She shot up. Ran over to the kitchen door. She had to get Dad down here. She had to get him down here and she had to get out of here and she had to get to Hollins and...

And then she saw something that made the hairs on the back of her neck stand on end.

Four people. Two men, two women.

All standing at the door.

All staring at her. Dead-eyed.

And then all running towards her.

She turned around instinctively. She needed—she needed to run. She didn't have time to stay here. She didn't even have time to warn Dad. She—she needed to get away. She needed to run. She needed to—

Suddenly, a force slammed into her right side.

Knocked her down to the hard kitchen floor.

She hit the floor with a crack. Slammed her head against it.

And then she turned around onto her side and tried to—tried to get away, tried to escape, tried to...

A man pinned her down.

Blood dripping from his eyes.

Thick, yellow saliva dangling down from his nostrils, and from his lips.

He opened his mouth.

Growled right at her.

And then he opened his mouth even wider, and wrapped his teeth around her neck, and all Keira could do was scream.

DWAYNE

* * *

Dwayne watched Nisha run through the fence and across the street and he couldn't actually believe what in the name of Christ he was witnessing.

She was running. Running across that damned road, as fast as she could. By her side... those bastards, ripping that poor soul to pieces right beneath them. Shit. She—she was trying to get to her dad. She was trying to get home. And he got that. He really got that.

But...

This. This was suicide.

He took a step through the gap in the fence. He couldn't just leave her. He had to catch her. He had to stop her. She was going to get herself killed. She was going to get caught and she was going to get bitten and...

Two of those figures stood up. And then another two. And then they all started running towards Nisha, running after her, following her, chasing her.

He stopped. Stood there. Heart racing. Shaking. Actually shaking. Why did he feel like this? This kid, she wasn't his responsibility. He barely even knew her. He wanted to find Mum. Mum. She—she was his responsibility. Finding her was his duty. That's what he had to do. Not... not protecting this kid. Protecting this kid who he barely even knew. A kid he'd almost died for already.

And it was her own stupid fault for running off. There was only so much helping a kid like that. He wanted to help her home. But he couldn't get home. So he was going to take her along with him to the care home, where he could focus on finding Mum. On getting her out of there.

But...

He looked up at Nisha. She ran across the road, almost tumbling over, almost losing her footing. She looked over her shoulder. Fear in her wide eyes. Then turned back to the houses, ran up the road, over towards the front door of a house on the left.

And then she—she opened that door. She opened that door and she ran inside and...

And then four other infected stood up. Ran off in that vague direction. Only... only they ran into another house. They ran into another house. And all Dwayne could do was stand there. All he could do was listen to those snarls. And all he could do was stare down the street, as the silence surrounded him.

He stood there. Shaking. He could barely breathe for the knots in his stomach. He needed to go into that house. He needed—he needed to go after her. He needed to find her. And he needed to know she was okay.

And then...

He thought of Mum.

Sitting there. Sitting there, upright in bed. Smelling the smoke. Listening to the screams. Seeing all the blood. He pictured how confused she would be. How afraid she would be. And he knew he'd stalled far too much already.

He needed to go after her. He needed to find her. He couldn't wait around any longer.

He looked around. Down the side of the fencing, further along the building site. He saw the taller buildings in the distance. Mum was over that way. She was so close. So close, and yet... and yet still so far away.

But he could get to her. He could get to her in no time at all. He could be there, in no time at all.

And then he heard a shout. A shout, from one of the houses. A... a scream? Nisha's scream? No. No, he didn't think Nisha could scream like that. She could barely speak, let alone scream.

But... what if?

His heart raced. His chest tightened. He closed his burning eyes, and he swallowed a lump in his throat.

He thought about that kid. About how he'd helped her. And about... about how she'd helped *him,* too.

And then he took another deep breath.

Because every time he thought of that girl, every time he thought about going after her, which instinct screamed at him to do... he thought of Mum.

He felt his jaw tensing. He squeezed his fists. And even though he knew it wasn't the right thing to do, even though he knew it would haunt him for the rest of his life... he knew he only had once choice.

He'd failed Mum one too many times already. He wasn't ready to fail her again.

He looked back over his shoulder. Back in the direction of Nisha. He thought about how he'd helped her. How she'd helped him—*saved* him. And then he thought about the decision she'd taken. The decision to run across the road. The decision to race after her dad.

He took a deep breath.

She'd made her choice. And now he had to make his.

He turned around, and he walked.

It was time to find Mum.

It was time to save her.

No matter what.

HELEN

* * *

W hen Helen saw Pete standing there, blood oozing down his face, she got this horrible, instinctive feeling in the pit of her stomach that she was in grave, grave danger.

It was the look in his eyes. The way his eyelids twitched. The way the blood trickled down his face. For a moment, for just a moment, she thought he might be bitten. He was one of those monsters, like the one who'd thrown itself in through her patio window. And like—like Carla and the kids, banging on the farmhouse window.

And then he narrowed his eyes, and he spoke, and she knew it was him, oh God it was him, and he was still here, and he'd chased her, and he—he was going to take her back to the house and he was...

Shit. What was that feeling she felt? That feeling she felt right in the pit of her stomach just looking at him? Was it... was it disappointment? Disappointment that he was still alive? Disappointment that he'd made it?

Whatever it was, Pete was the last person she wanted to see right now.

"All this time," he said, staring right into her eyes. "All these years. I bet you've—I bet you've been fucking him, haven't you? I bet you were fucking him the whole time."

Helen glanced around at Farmer John. He was sobbing away. Inside the house, Carla and the kids banged on the window. Blood oozed from Carla's lips. And blood oozed from a bite wound on John's arm.

"I just wanted to protect them," John muttered. "I just—I just wanted to protect them."

A knot tightened in Helen's stomach. John had been bitten. Soon, he was going to change. He was going to change, just like Carla had changed, and just like so many people on Twitter reported changing. So she wasn't safe. She wasn't safe, stood here, right next to him.

But somehow, she felt safer standing here next to John than she felt anywhere near Pete.

Pete took a step towards her. His fists were clenched. He looked like a man possessed. The man she'd met all those years ago—the man she'd fallen in love with all those years ago—so sensitive, so tender, so gentle, that man was gone now. That man died to her a long time ago, sure. But in his place, right now? An angry, bitter man who looked like he'd stop at nothing to get what he wanted.

Hell might hath no fury where a woman's scorned. But a *man* scorned? Yeah. That was hell itself.

"I just wanted to protect them," John gasped.

Pete narrowed his eyes. He walked even closer towards Helen. Muttering things under his breath. Saliva and blood dangled down from his lips. He looked a man possessed.

And then Helen saw something. Something caught her eye, right there on the ground. The shotgun. John's shotgun. Lying there, beside him.

Could she?

She didn't want to *shoot* Pete. Or... or maybe she did. Maybe she *did* want to shoot him. At least if she shot him, she didn't have to worry about him anymore. If she shot him... if she shot him, she could just say when things went back to normal that she had nothing to do with it; that he must've got bitten, that he must've got turned, or that something awful must've happened to him, and—

No. No, why was she even thinking like this? What the hell was going on in her head.

Pete took another step towards her. "Look at you. You hit me. You leave me for dead. And you go running off to John. Pathetic. Totally pathetic."

Helen shook her head. "Don't do this, Pete. We're... done. And you've... You killed Billy. You killed him. I love him, and you killed him—"

"You love *me!*" Pete shouted.

Birds flapped away from nearby trees. Pete's shout echoed around this silent farmyard. And she could hear that anguish in his voice. That sheer desperate anguish in his cry.

And all she could think about?

All she could think about was how much she hated him.

And how much she pitied what he'd become.

She went to open her mouth when a smash split through the silence.

Followed by a snarl, and a scream.

Shit. Oh, shit. It came from the farmhouse. It came from...

"Carla?" John said. "Kids? Stay inside. It's not safe out here. It's..."

And Helen didn't hear what else John said. He let go of her and he ran over towards Carla, towards his kids.

They were out of the house. And they were running towards John.

She looked at Pete. Pete stood there. Wide-eyed. Staring at the commotion. And Helen saw that shotgun on the ground, right at her feet. This was it. This was her moment. This was her opportunity. This was her chance.

She knew what she had to do.

Pete turned around.

Looked into her eyes.

And then down at the shotgun.

"You wouldn't..." he muttered.

Helen launched down.

Grabbed the shotgun.

Lifted and pointed it at Pete, her hands shaking.

"Not another step," she gasped.

Pete raised his hands. His smile widened. "You wouldn't dare."

Helen looked around. John, running towards his family. "You were supposed to stay inside! It's not safe for you out here! It's not —argh!"

And then they dragged him down. They dragged him down to the ground, and they bit his arms, and they bit his legs, and they bit his stomach. Blood oozed out, all over the grass. Into the pond, turning it red.

"Please!" he screamed. "Please!"

And Helen stood there. Shotgun in hand. Focused on Pete. Eyes stinging. Ears ringing with Pete's agonised cries. "Not another step."

Pete lowered his hands.

His smile widened.

"You wouldn't dare," he said.

She saw Carla in the corner of her eyes. Lifting her head. Looking vacantly in their direction. Turning her interest from her poor husband, over towards her and Pete.

And then she saw Pete taking another step, as the kids looked up, as they all looked over.

"You wouldn't dream of—"

And then Helen did something she didn't think she was capable of, as the family raced across the garden, and towards their position.

She pointed at Pete's left knee.

And she pulled the trigger.

DAVID

* * *

David heard the scream downstairs and he felt like he was being punched in the stomach.

Keira. It was her. He knew it was her. He recognised that scream. He'd heard it before, so many times. He'd heard it on rollercoasters on Blackpool Pleasure Beach, when they were going down the big drop on the Big One that day. He'd heard her scream when he made her jump, when he jumped out of her wardrobe one afternoon. And he'd heard that scream when she accidentally walked in on him and Rina watching The Mummy, which wasn't even all that scary—something they always teased her about.

He'd heard that scream another time, too.

A time he didn't want to think about.

A memory he didn't want to revisit.

A place he didn't want to go. Not again.

He dropped this Nisha kid's school bag and without even thinking, he ran to the bedroom door, ran out onto the landing, ran towards the stairs, while downstairs, he heard screaming, he heard gasping, he heard...

And then he felt the ground disappearing from under his feet.

He tumbled. Rolled down the stairs. Behind him, Rufus barked, as David rolled down the stairs and collided with the wall beside the door. He turned over, onto his back, his head aching, his mouth filled with the taste of blood. That screaming. That gasping. It was—it was close. It was in the hallway. It was...

He looked up and he saw something that sent shivers down his spine.

Keira. Keira was lying on the floor. There was someone on top of her. A man on top of her. Pushing her down.

And he had his teeth around her shoulder.

David didn't even think.

He stood up and he ran across the hallway. He ran, as he listened to Rufus barking upstairs. He ran, even though he could hear more gasping and more growling in this house, even though he knew they weren't alone in here.

He tackled the man, side-on. Ripped him away from Keira. He pinned him down and he punched him in the face. Hard. Then he punched him again, and again, as the man gasped and growled and tried to scratch David's face and tried to snap at him with his teeth.

But David just kept on punching him.

Just kept on hitting him.

Hitting him harder, and harder, and harder, banging his head against the wooden floor, watching it bleed, hearing it crack, and—

A shove. A shove, right behind him. And then before he knew it, *he* was the one on the floor. He was the one on the floor with someone on top of him. A woman, this time. Her eyes were red. Her face was pale. And her teeth cracked against each other, so hard they sounded like they were one the verge of splitting to pieces completely.

David held her back. He pushed her back, trying to keep her jaws away from him. But—but she was strong. And she was manic. She bit at the air widely, like a rabid animal. And in a way, that's what she was. That's exactly what she was. A rabid animal. There was nothing human in her eyes. Whatever she was suffering, whatever she was going through, there was nothing *human* in there anymore.

He pressed her back when suddenly he felt her nails in his throat. Damned false nails. Why the hell did women have to go and get false nails? They really weren't very bloody convenient right now.

She inched towards his face. Her jaw snapped. Her teeth cracked together. She was so close to biting him. She was so close to sinking her teeth into him.

But at least he'd helped Keira.

At least he'd helped his girl.

That was all he could hope for.

He closed his eyes as this monstrous bitch bit the air inches from his face.

As Rufus's barks filled the house.

As the gasps and the growls and the cries grew louder, and louder, and...

A bang.

A bang. Right above his head.

He opened his eyes.

The woman. She was still staring at him with those empty eyes. But... but she was bleeding. Bleeding from the back of her head.

She tumbled to David's side, twitching. Spluttering. Coughing up blood.

And when David looked up... he saw what'd happened.

Keira. Standing there. A bloody iron in hand. Eyes wide. And staring down at the woman she'd just hit.

David dragged himself up to his feet. He grabbed Keira's hand, as she stood there, shaking, dazed.

"I—I killed her," Keira muttered.

"Come on," David said.

"I hit her. I—"

"We can talk about this outside," he said. "The school. The kid. Hollins—"

"Hollins Primary School," Keira said.

She looked at him. And he looked back at her. And for a moment, for just a moment, he felt like her dad again. He felt like she was his daughter again. He saw that look of longing in her eyes, that look of vulnerability, that look of *wanting* him to be there, *wanting* him to look out for her, *wanting* him to be her father... and he felt it. He felt it, right to his core.

And then he heard another gasp.

He looked around. More of those bastards. Running off the street, and into this house. Rufus standing between them. Growling. Barking.

He looked back at Keira, at his girl, and that momentary vulnerability had dropped away entirely now.

But it was still there. He'd seen it. It was there, so he could make it work.

"Come on," he said.

He grabbed her hand.

She held his hand back. Loosely.

And then, with Rufus closely in tow, they ran out, through the back door of the house, out into the yard, and towards whatever awaited them out in the dangerous unknown.

NISHA

* * *

Nisha ran away from Dwayne and towards her home and she tried not to think about the bad people ripping the man apart in the middle of the road.

She saw her home, right ahead. She thought of Dad. Dad, hiding inside there, waiting for her. He'd be so proud of her when she walked through the front door. He'd hug her and he'd laugh and he'd keep her safe. He'd keep her safe from all the bad people, and all the monsters, and it wouldn't be like a bad dream anymore. She could get through *anything* when Dad was there.

She looked at her house in the distance and she felt tingling in her belly. Her legs were frozen solid. She was running fast, as fast as she could run, but she felt like it wasn't fast enough. She was never good at sports day. Dad always told her she was really quick, and she could beat him in a race, but when she took part in races on sports day she always came near the back and it made her realise Dad was lying, just to make her happy. Which annoyed her more, in a way.

She didn't want someone pretending she was strong. Or fast. She wanted to *be* strong, and fast.

Right now she just ran and ran as fast as she could across the street and tried not to look back, tried not to think about the bad people in the road, tried not to think about them chasing her, she just tried to think about home, and how close she was, how close to Dad she was, how close to this whole nightmare ending she was, and...

Home.

Right opposite her.

Only...

The door was open.

The front door was open, and—

People. People, inside.

A woman. A woman she didn't recognise, lying there on the floor. And—and someone else on top of her. Pinning her down.

Nisha stared at the woman on the floor. Who was this woman, in her home? Was—was she one of Dad's friends? She didn't know who she was. But—but she was in danger. She was in danger, and...

She only just realised at that moment that she'd stopped running. She'd stopped moving altogether. She was frozen. Frozen to the spot.

She didn't want to look back. She didn't want to look over her shoulder. But she did. She turned and she looked over her shoulder, towards the bad people.

They... they were chasing her. Running towards her. Three of them. All of them, racing after her. They all had bloody faces. They all had angry eyes. And they were all running so, so fast. Faster than she could run.

She turned around and she saw movement. Movement, in her home. Bad people? More bad people? She wasn't sure. She didn't know. She—she just had to run. She had to move. She couldn't stand here. And—and home. Home was too dangerous. She couldn't go home. She needed something else. She needed some*where* else.

She saw the house next door. Mrs Halloway's house. She was always nice. Always kind. Always gave Nisha lollipops, even when Dad told her she shouldn't eat too many lollipops 'cause they'd rot her teeth.

Maybe she'd be home. She was always home. Maybe—maybe she could help. She really hoped she could help. And—and when things got better, when things got quieter, she could go back home and see if she could find Dad.

She ran. Ran towards Mrs Halloway's. She kept on looking ahead. One good thing about not being able to hear was that she couldn't hear the bad people running after her right now. Which meant she could focus. She could concentrate.

Just get to Mrs Halloway's.

Just get to Mrs Halloway's, and everything would be okay.

She stumbled on a crack in the road. Almost fell over. Steadied herself, then started running again. She was okay. Everything was going to be okay.

She ran down Mrs Halloway's front garden path. She slammed the front gate behind her. She looked back. Some of those people were running towards her home now. But two of them were still following her. And they were so close.

She turned back around. Ran up to Mrs Halloway's front door. She always kept it open. She always kept it unlocked. Dad always told her she should lock her front door 'cause there were bad people around, people who'd steal from her, people who'd hurt her, people who'd "take advantage" of her, whatever that meant.

She grabbed the handle. Tried to turn it.

Her stomach sank.

It was locked.

She tried again. Tried turning it. But—but it wasn't moving. It wasn't moving and—and the bad people. The bad people were so close. The bad people were getting closer. One of them, a bald

man, jumped over the gate, tripping over and landing on the ground. The other pushed the gate open. Ran down the path, ran towards Nisha.

She turned around and she closed her eyes and she banged on the door.

Hard.

She banged, as they got closer to her, and she thought about the kitchen. The kitchen, where the bad people surrounded her, but didn't attack her. And the school toilets. Mrs Thompson. Holding her. Moving towards her, snapping her teeth together. But then... letting her go.

She thought about them, and even though she knew something was weird about it—something was different about her—maybe she was wrong. Maybe she'd just been lucky. Because they were coming for her. They were coming for her, and they were going to get her. They were going to tear her apart.

She banged on Mrs Halloway's front door again, and she waited for them to slam into her, and she closed her burning eyes and she thought of Dad.

Please.

Please be okay.

I'm almost home, Dad. I'm almost home.

Please be—

And then she felt the hands grabbing her back, and in her head, she screamed.

PETE

* * *

Pete watched Helen pull the trigger and his entire *world* stood still.

She stood there. Staring at him. Pointing that shotgun at him. Tears streamed down her cheeks. Her eyes bulged wide. She looked angry. She looked sad. She looked... desperate.

Shouting filled the silence. Screaming. Farmer John, pleading with his family—with his own damned family—as they bit chunks out of him. "Please! I—I wanna help! I wanna—It's me. Please. Please!"

And hearing him brought Pete no joy. Even though he didn't *like* the prick, it brought him no joy at all, as he stood there. The metallic scent of blood filling the air. And this... this weird earthiness. Like a graveyard. A graveyard on a warm, rainy day. A smell unlike anything he'd ever smelled.

Like... like death warmed up. Literally.

But—but suddenly, John's family weren't biting him anymore. They were looking up. Up at Pete. Up at Helen.

And Helen was standing there. Pointing that shotgun at him.

"You wouldn't," Pete said.

And then she lowered the shotgun.

Pointed it towards his legs.

And...

She pulled the trigger.

He waited for the blast. He waited for the sudden burst of pain—a dull ache, growing stronger, and stronger, and stronger. He waited to fall to the floor in a heap, as right in front of him, he looked into the eyes of a woman he'd once loved, a woman who once loved *him*, and he saw nothing but pure hatred.

But Pete didn't hear a blast.

And he didn't feel any pain, either.

He just heard... a click.

A click of a trigger.

And then nothing.

Helen's eyes widened. She looked down at the shotgun. Then back up at Pete. "What..."

And then it hit Pete. Not pain. Quite the goddamned opposite. *Realisation*. That's what hit Pete.

The realisation that there were no shells in that shotgun. Of course there weren't. Of course there weren't. It was for display. It was to scare kids away. There weren't any damned shells at all. Only... hadn't he heard a bang before? Hell, maybe there was only the one shell in there. Or maybe the gun had failed. Maybe he'd got lucky. Very damned lucky.

But Helen tried again.

She backed away, and she pulled that trigger again. And again. Every desperate click after desperate click, music to Pete's ears. Painful music.

Because those clicks showed him just how much she detested him.

He heard the snarls beside him.

He heard the gasps, inching closer.

He looked around. Carla and the kids, all running towards him, towards Helen.

He looked back around at Helen. And even though he was in danger, even though he was in deep shit... he smiled.

She stared back at him. Pale-faced. Wide-eyed.

And then she ran.

Pete ran after her. His head ached. His muscles felt weak. Running wasn't easy. Running wasn't easy at all.

But he ran. And he kept on running.

He had to get away from the infected.

And he had to catch Helen.

She ran down the path in front of the farmhouse. Glanced over her shoulder, almost losing her footing. He just stared at her. Ran after her. Closed in on her. Like a predator. A predator closing in on its prey.

Only... well, she was no prey. She wasn't innocent. She'd hit him over the head. And then she'd tried to shoot him. And sure. Sure, he might've killed her wet lettuce of a partner. But he was doing her a favour there anyway. In the long run, he was doing her a favour. She didn't need that creep around. She needed him. Him, and only him.

She looked back again. Staggered again. Almost tumbled over. And then she screamed. She screamed, and even though Pete could hear the gasps and the growls and the cries behind him of the oncoming family of infected bastards, he smiled. She was his. And she was afraid. Good. That's what she deserved. That fear was *exactly* what she deserved.

She turned back ahead. Ran past the opening down towards Tim and Mary's place. Tim and Mary were a pair of sour-faced pricks too. And Pete wouldn't have a problem dealing with them if he had to get to Helen. Tim was a complete fucking tool. A weak little shit who didn't have a single bone in his spine. If Pete walked up to him, flashed his badge, he'd hand Helen right over in a flash. Little creep.

But Helen didn't run down there. She kept on running down the road. Her mistake. John's family were on their tail. And somehow... somehow he didn't give a shit if they caught up with him and Helen right now. If they were going down, they were going down together. They were...

A flash. A sudden flash, in his mind's eye. A flash of the good times with Helen. A flash of the laughter on that Spanish beach. A flash of sitting in front of the telly together, full of a cold on Christmas Day, and having the nicest, cosiest time. And a flash of... of their wedding. Looking into her eyes and seeing the most beautiful woman in the world, walking down the aisle towards him.

And... and he felt guilty. As he ran down the road, after her, seeing the fear in her eyes—the fear not just at the oncoming infected, but the fear at *him,* too... that was soul-crushing. Completely soul-crushing. What'd happened to him? He didn't used to be a monster. He didn't used to be violent. What—what had he done?

He looked over his shoulder. John's family, right behind him. And then he looked ahead at Helen. And suddenly he didn't see this woman he detested. Suddenly, he saw the woman he loved. He'd hurt her. He'd hurt her so bad. And—and what he'd done to Billy, what he'd done to the man she loved... fuck. That—that was awful. He—he didn't mean to do it. There was just the trauma: the trauma of today, the trauma of everything he'd seen, of everything that'd happened, all of it bottling up, and...

He saw Helen falling.

Saw her slipping.

Saw her tripping up.

And in his mind's eye... he saw himself leaving her. Saw her screaming. Saw her pleading. Begging him to stay. Begging him to help.

He felt some awful momentary satisfaction about that.

And then he ran over to her, and grabbed her, and dragged her up from the road.

And then he threw himself and her into the bushes by the side of the infected.

The pair of them fell. Hit the ground. And then he stood up. Held out a hand to Helen, as the infected family scrambled at the hedge to get through; to break through.

"Come on," he said. Holding out his shaking hand.

Helen looked around. Around at the hedge. Around at the farmer's family, and then back at Pete.

"Come on," Pete said. Extending his hand again. "We—we don't have much time. We don't have…"

And then he saw it in slow motion.

Helen.

Grabbing his hand.

The warmth of her hand in his, for just a solitary moment.

Her. Standing there. Standing right in front of him.

"I'm sorry."

And then the momentary confusion. Sorry? Sorry for what? For Billy? For trying to shoot him? For hitting him? Because that was okay. It was all okay. 'Cause he loved her. She was his wife and he loved her. He loved her so much.

And then she pushed him back into the bush.

Into the clutches of the infected.

KEIRA

* * *

Keira waked down the street with Dad and this dog, Rufus, and couldn't shake the sense of tension splitting through the air.

It might only be a few hours since the outbreak spilled over, but the hustle and bustle of the streets had been replaced by an eerie silence, broken only by distant sounds of chaos and occasional cries for help. The quiet emptiness amplified their every footstep, weighing Keira's awareness of the surrounding danger.

Abandoned cars cluttered the streets. Some of them had crashed into one another, while others were left haphazardly parked across the road. Remnants of hastily discarded belongings covered the street, along with scattered debris—handbags, mobile phones, all sorts of things.

But it wasn't all misery, as Keira walked along the street, towards Nisha's school. That's what she kept on telling herself. They had a chance. A chance of getting to Hollins Primary School. Of finding Nisha there. And of getting Nisha away from there. Of looking after her. And besides. Hours had passed now.

Which meant... Well, it meant *someone* had to be out there, preparing to help everyone, didn't they? The government would soon step in. The police. The military. Someone would help them. And once Keira found Nisha, once she got her to safety... it would only be a matter of time before someone stepped in. Someone instilled a sense of order.

And besides. After the initial chaos on the streets, Keira saw more glimmers of hope. Small groups of survivors, banding together amidst the chaos. Families. Groups of families, gathered in front gardens. A couple of blokes erecting tall fences around their houses, ushering people behind them. People looking out for each other. People helping each other. A sense of community —a flicker of light amidst the horrible darkness.

But every time she saw those glimmers of hope... Keira felt a flicker of fear in her stomach, and in her chest. The violence she'd witnessed. The chaos at the hospital. The total disarray. Jean. Gavin. Omar. They weren't coming back. They were... they were dead, and they weren't coming back. And it didn't matter how much communities came together, how much they banded together, and it didn't matter how much solidarity they showed. People had died. And that trauma—the trauma of what she'd witnessed, the trauma of what so many had witnessed—that wasn't ever going to go away.

A distant scream made Keira flinch. And it was this fear that haunted her. This constant tension, this constant state of anxiety, preparing for whatever potential threats might be around the corner. The fear of encountering more infected individuals, or desperate survivors... it all just added to the tension of their journey. And it was growing unbearable.

She looked around at the broken windows. The boarded-up shops. The once vibrant and lively neighbourhood appeared forlorn, neglected, even though it'd only been a matter of hours since the shit truly hit the fan. It was like lockdown all over again, only far more extreme, far more pronounced, and far more... terrifying. Because there was no preparing for this. There was no news filtering slowly from other countries. There was no highly anticipated Boris Johnson lockdown announcement. There was just... death. Death, and violence, and chaos, and a nation tumbling out of control.

She looked around. Dad walked beside her. He looked from left to right at all times, constantly monitoring his surroundings. He looked at her, and he half-smiled. She half-smiled back at him, then looked away. She didn't want to look at him for too long. It made her stomach feel... weird. She just had to focus on the road. Focus on reaching Nisha's school. Focus on—

"I don't like this," Dad said.

Keira's stomach sank. Here it was... "Don't like what?"

Dad nodded ahead. "This. Any of this. We shouldn't be doing this."

"There's someone I've got to—"

"Help. Someone you made a promise to. I get that. I understand. But we... we barely made it out of her dad's place alive. You've seen how dangerous shit is. We both have. We've got to be careful now. So careful. We..."

A scream echoed from a street ahead, stopping Dad in his tracks. He looked around, then back at Keira, raising his eyebrows, as if to prove a point.

Keira's cheeks flushed. "You don't have to be here."

"I told you. That's a non-negotiable."

"Because you're such a good, ever-present dad."

"You were the one who cut ties with me," Dad said. "Not the other way round."

Keira stopped. "Really? That's the way you see it?"

Dad shrugged. His cheeks glowed red, like they always did when he was pissed off. "You could've talked to me."

"I didn't *want* to talk to you," Keira said. "Anyway. This... this really isn't the time."

"We can talk and walk."

"We're trying to get to a school in the middle of some kind of killer virus outbreak. I think... I think we're better focusing. Concentrating. Because I'm not mad keen on getting torn apart today."

She looked away. Kept walking. Shit. Maybe she was being too harsh. Maybe she was being awkward. He—he was just worried about her. He was just expressing concern. She was his daughter at the end of the day.

And as much as she didn't want to admit it to herself... didn't he have a point?

"I won't ever stop apologising for what happened that day," Dad said. "For... for not being there. And for... for freezing. When I did. For... for how distant I went afterwards. For not being there for you. For not being a good father. It'll haunt me. It'll haunt me for the rest of my life. I was a bad dad. But I... I just want an opportunity, Keira. I just want... a chance. A chance to be better. A chance to do things right."

Keira looked around at him. His words, they made a lump swell up in her throat. The tears in his eyes took her back. Took her right back. The accident. Driving in that car, Mum by her side. Mum's laughter. A Stereophonics song she always loved playing on the radio. The pair of them, singing along. But... but something wasn't right. Mum. She was crying about something. Her and Dad, they'd been arguing. They'd been arguing about— about some woman at work. Some woman at work who Dad was getting a bit too close to. And they kept talking about papers, and about moving house, and about all kinds of things that Keira just wanted to bury her head in the sand about and not think about.

Dad was meant to be picking Keira up from school. But he was late. So late that all the other mums and dads had taken their kids home, and Mrs Rigby had to ring Mum to come pick her up. And she remembered *knowing* the second she saw Mum that she was mad. With her? She wasn't sure. She didn't think so. It felt... it felt more like she was mad with someone else. Mad with Dad.

She remembered sitting there in that car, and seeing the car driving on the wrong side of the road, and thinking it looked weird. And she remembered looking at Mum, and Mum looking at her, smiling, laughing, tearful eyes.

And then she remembered the bang.

The bang.

The smash.

The explosion.

After that... she remembered the taste of blood. She remembered the screaming. The screaming was the worst part. The screaming was the part she tried to forget more than anything else. Mum's screaming. Stretching out her bloodied hand and staring at Keira as blood and guts spilled out of her split chest and belly, and crying out in pain.

"Please," she gasped, as she pushed her phone towards Keira. "Dad. Ring. Please."

And Keira felt the tears stinging her eyes, as she returned to present day. As she looked up at the man who'd been too busy having an affair to answer his phone. At the haunted look on his face, as he stood there, frozen, just as he'd frozen that day. Frozen when the news finally got to him. Frozen, when he ran out into the street. Frozen, as his world fell apart.

"I can't forgive," Keira said. "I... I can't. But you can help me find Nisha. If that's what you're willing to do."

Dad opened his mouth. Then he closed it. So pale. So dishevelled. So *haunted*.

And then he nodded.

He looked like he was about to apologise. Yet another apology. And then he just looked into her eyes and half-smiled back at her. "I can do that."

She nodded back at him. Back at this man who she knew loved her dearly. A man who loved Mum, but betrayed Mum. A man who'd been served the most awful dish of suffering imaginable for his sins.

And then she turned around and she saw it, right in the distance.

The grey-brick walls.

The empty car park.

The fields, and the football nets.

She swallowed a lump in her throat.

Hollins Primary School.

She was here.

They'd made it.

DWAYNE

* * *

Dwayne walked towards his mum's care home and tried not to think about the girl he'd left behind.

Distant screams echoed through the streets. Every one he heard, he thought of Nisha. He pictured her, lying there, the infected on top of her. Pinning her down. Sinking their teeth into her neck. He pictured her wide eyes. Her hands, reaching out, grasping for help. Shit. He'd left her. He'd let her run away. And if anything happened to her... that was on him.

He shook his head. He couldn't think that way. He'd helped Nisha. He'd saved her, when she needed saving. And she'd returned the favour. Now... now, they'd gone their separate ways. That's all there was to it. He was going after Mum, and she was going after her dad. Besides. She'd done a runner. She'd gone against his advice and she'd done a runner, right onto that infected-filled street. What was he supposed to do? Go running after her? No. He barely knew the kid. He barely knew her. And grateful as he was to her for helping him, for being so brave... their journey had reached its end.

Their journey. Why was he even thinking in those terms? What'd happened to that cold interior he was so good at hiding? Because he *was* cold. He was cold to the core. That's what everyone told him, anyway. Everyone he worked with. Dwayne. Doesn't give a shit. Good at pretending he gives a shit to get what he wants, but scratch beneath the surface a little and you find... ice.

So why was he so guilty about leaving that kid behind?

He shook his head. Took a deep breath. Nico would be taking the piss out of him right now. *A kid? You gave up that cold heart of yours for a kid?*

He thought of Nico. His stomach sank. As much as he saw him as a colleague, as a partner in crime, and as much as he tried not to make any sort of connection with the people he worked with... he had to admit he felt shitty about what'd happened to Nico. The way he'd died. The way he'd sat there in that driver's seat, transformed, and then turned into one of those monsters. He pitied him, somehow. He was just trying to make a better life for himself. A better life for his family. He was just trying to repay the last of his debts, just like Dwayne. And he was so close to an exit. So close to a way out, once and for all.

And now he was... now he was one of those *things.*

Was it reversible, this disease? It was hard to see how it could be. Some of the wounds people had... those wounds weren't *survivable* wounds. So even if someone somehow *did* manage to reverse the anger... it wasn't like they could suddenly turn them into the average Joe. The blood loss. The organ damage. You didn't recover from that shit overnight. You didn't recover from that shit *ever.*

And it hit Dwayne, then, as he walked further down this street, further away from Nisha, and closer towards Mum's care home. Whatever was happening... it was unlike anything that'd ever happened before. Ever. At no other time in history had people suddenly turned into these rage-fuelled beasts. At no other time in history had people been able to keep on going with wounds like some of the ones he'd seen; with blood loss like he'd seen.

It was a new world. And it felt like Dwayne had been living in it far, far longer than he knew he had.

He walked further down the road. Kept his head down. He didn't want to look at the houses. He didn't want to see people, hiding behind their curtains, peeking out at the terror outside. He didn't want to see the abandoned cars. And he didn't want to see any more signs that the city was falling apart, all around him.

He just wanted to find Mum. And then he could think about the next step. Whatever the next step was.

Suddenly, he heard a noise overhead. A plane, flying low, hurtling past. It was flying way too low for Preston. The sound was earth-shaking. And... and was that smoke he saw? Smoke, spouting from one of the wings? What in the name of fuck was going on?

He looked away. Turned back to the road. Looked down the street. Abandoned cars. Shops with shutters down. People running by, screaming. No signs of community. No signs of togetherness, not even here in the suburbs. Just panic. Fear. And a total sense of confusion.

And with every step he took, with every attempt he made to exorcise Nisha from his mind... he couldn't stop thinking of her. Again, and again, and again.

He wasn't sure how long he'd been walking when he finally saw it, right there in the distance.

On the left, the school.

But on the right... on the right, the place he'd been looking for. The place he'd been heading towards. The place he'd been working towards, all day long.

The care home.

Mum.

He looked back. Back over his shoulder. Back down the road.

He saw the smoke. He heard the screams. He tasted the salt on his lips, and he smelled the rusty metal and burning plastic, and he thought of Nisha.

A knot tightened, right in the middle of his stomach.

"I'm sorry," he said.

And then he turned around and he ran towards the care home.

HELEN

* * *

Helen pushed Pete into the bushes, and then she turned around and ran across the field.

She heard the groaning behind her. The snarling. The gasping. And—and she heard something else, too. Crying out in pain. She tried not to think about where that crying was coming from; about *who* that crying was coming from. But in her mind's eye, she couldn't escape him. She couldn't get rid of the image of his face.

Pete.

A man she once loved.

A man she now sorely, sorely detested for what he'd done to her.

For what he'd taken from her.

The image of him. Standing there. Looking into her eyes. Looking at her with... with this pitiful expression on his face. This *loving* expression on his face.

Even after everything, he still had that pitiful, loving expression on his face.

And then she'd pushed him into the bushes, into the clutching hands of the infected.

And now she ran.

She ran across the field. She could see the road up ahead, in the distance. She—she just needed to get there. She just needed to get away from this field and get to that road. Because—because if she got to that road then she was free. If she got to that road then she could get away and she could—she could go far, far away, and...

A scream. Right behind her. A scream belonging to a man she recognised.

"Helen!"

Pete. That pitiful scream. Tears welled up in her eyes. She didn't want to look over her shoulder. She didn't want to go back. Because—because Pete was a monster. He'd *killed* Billy. He'd killed the man she loved. So she couldn't go back. No, she couldn't go back. Had to keep going. Had to keep running. Had to keep—

"Please!"

And she felt her knees weakening, wobbling. She felt tears streaming down her face. Because even though Pete was a monster, even though he'd done such horrible things to her, and even though he'd clearly lost his mind... she felt guilty.

She wanted to go back. She wanted to help him.

She didn't want to leave him to the infected.

She looked back. And when she looked back, over by those bushes she'd pushed him, she didn't see him. She just saw... movement. Shuffling movement. Was he gone? Had they taken him already? Had they bitten him? Shit. Shit, shit, shit. She wasn't that person. She wasn't vengeful. She was... she was a good person. She was a good person and she'd never done anything wrong in her life. In her whole damned life she'd never done anything wrong. Nothing major, anyway. Nothing *illegal*.

She stood there in the middle of this field in the middle of the countryside and she saw smoke in the distance. Smoke, rising from town. She could smell it, too. Smell it in the air. Burning. Burning, and sweat, and blood.

She looked back. Back towards those bushes. The movement. The shuffling. And the distant snarling. If she went back there... she was dead. If she went back there, she was finished. If she went back there, then she was consigning herself to a death sentence. And for what? For who?

For Pete.

For the man who'd killed Billy.

For the man who wanted to *possess* her.

A man who had changed, so so much.

Did she want to sacrifice her own life for him?

Or was there more to her life?

More *for* her life?

She stood there, under the clouds, and she swallowed a lump in her sore throat. She wiped her eyes. She took a deep breath. She didn't know where to go. She didn't know what she was going to do. But she knew she couldn't go back to those bushes. She couldn't go back for Pete. And she couldn't go back home, either.

She reached for her phone, and felt a gap where her phone should be. Shit. She'd left it at home. She'd left it at home and she wasn't going back there. She wasn't going back there and seeing Billy, lying there. And even if she did... even if she did, her phone service had cut off just before Pete arrived. A constant tone, whoever she tried to call.

She thought of her parents. Up in Lancaster. She—she could walk there, if she had to. It was a long way. But did she have a choice? Besides. Maybe... maybe she'd run into help on the way. Maybe someone would get this under control before she got there. They had to. Someone had to. There was no way this didn't come under control, somehow.

Right?

She stood there, dug her nails into her fingers, and she took another deep breath. She felt sick. Her stomach ached. Her head spun. She wanted to wake up. She wanted to wake up from this nightmare and for it all to be over. She wanted to wake up and hug Billy, tight. She wanted to look out of her window and not be worried about the possibility of Pete being out there.

She wanted... she wanted her parents.

She took a deep breath. Looked back at the bushes. The bushes she'd pushed Pete into.

And then she closed her burning eyes, and she turned around.

She looked at the road, right up ahead, and she walked.

She'd only walked a couple of steps when she swore she heard another scream, right behind her.

"Helen! Helen! Please..."

DAVID

* * *

David saw the school in the distance and a knot tightened in his stomach.

Because he was worried about what he was going to find there.

Or rather, what he was going to *fail* to find. Because somehow that seemed... a scarier concept.

He walked with Keira by his side, with Rufus between them. Rufus seemed happy enough. Trotting along. Wagging his tail. Blissfully oblivious to what he'd lost, just today. His owner. The nurse, back at Mrs Kirkham's place. He remembered the look on her face, the blood streaming down her cheeks, and the way she'd thrown herself at him, the way she'd attacked him and... and David wondered whether Rufus even registered something had changed. How much in the present did dogs actually live? They missed their owners, because they were always happy to see them again. But would he be pining for her now? It didn't seem that way.

He glanced up at Keira. He thought about the days, the

weeks, the months and the years he'd spent, wishing he was there for her. Wishing he was in contact with her again. Wishing he could make amends for the past. Time and time again.

He looked ahead at the school. To say it looked eerie was an understatement. There always was something eerie about schools when they were quiet. Of course, today should just be an ordinary school day. Kids went in today with no sense of the crisis and the chaos that was about to unfold in the world outside. But things were very different now. So much had changed, in such a short space of time. So much had changed that David knew damn well was never going to revert. It was going to be hard to put this damned genie back into the bottle, that was for sure.

There were hardly any cars in the car park out front. And there was an eerie silence to the school. Behind the windows... there was no movement. No movement whatsoever.

"Remember the drill," David said.

Keira rolled her eyes. "In and out. I get it."

David nodded. He looked around. Year Six. That's what year she was in. They were going to go into that classroom. They were going to search it. And then... and then they were going to do a quick sweep of the place and see if there were any signs of her. And if there weren't... they were getting out of here. Getting away from here.

And Keira agreed. Reluctantly, she agreed. But David worried that she was just agreeing for the sake of it. That she was just going along with what he was suggesting to keep him quiet, to keep him from protesting too much. Did she really have any intention at all of coming back with him, after all this? He couldn't imagine so.

He took a deep breath. Smelled the smoke in the air. Felt a cool breeze brush against his hot skin.

One step at a time.

They walked through the car park. The street opposite was eerie. Scarily so. When David looked up at the houses opposite the school, he saw figures in those windows. Peeking out. Watching him. That explained why the streets were so empty, then. People were staying home. They'd been told to stay at home, and after some initial reluctance—understandable post-pandemic lockdown scepticism—they were adhering. Because they'd seen the attacks. They'd seen just how violent this outbreak was—whatever the hell it was.

And now they were hiding in their homes and waiting for help.

David looked around at the abandoned cars. At the smashed windows. And at the blood, splattered across the pavements and the roads. Somehow, he figured they might be waiting a while. Where were the police? Where was the military? Was there some sort of recovery operation going on? Or... or were those individuals just as afraid and just as *decimated* as everyone else?

He looked back at the school. Took another deep breath. Keira walked ahead of him slightly. Walked down the pathway, towards the main entrance. It was dark behind those doors. There was no sign of anyone sitting at reception. The school looked... abandoned. It looked empty. And yet there was something about it. Something... *ominous* about it. A sense that behind those blinds, there were secrets awaiting them. Dark secrets. Things they didn't want to see. Things they didn't want to find.

"What if we don't find her?" David said. He didn't want to say those words. He was trying to repress them. He knew Keira didn't want to hear them. But he had to be honest. Brutally honest.

"We will," Keira said.

"But if we don't—"

"Then we keep trying, okay?" she said, her voice shaking. "We keep trying."

David swallowed a lump in his throat as they walked down the pathway, towards those doors. "You know... you're a caring soul. You always have been. But sometimes... sometimes, you can't save everyone."

"And that philosophy has got you far, has it?"

"You can think what you want about me," David said. "I know... I know what I did. I know I wasn't there for you when I should've been. And I know I... I know I failed Mum. But if I could've swapped places with her. If I could've been the one driving that day. If I could've died so she could live and so you... so you don't have to live with that trauma... then I would. I would. And I think about it every fucking minute of every fucking day."

He didn't know where it'd come from, this outburst. And it was the first time it'd ever happened, in front of Keira. He didn't usually like airing his emotions so openly. He'd apologised to Keira before. Of course he had. But this. This felt... different.

Because somehow, this openness was like an admission. An admission of his shame.

An admission of his guilt.

And an admission of how much he knew he'd failed this girl.

He couldn't look her in the eye. He couldn't look at her right now. He could only look past her. At the school. But when he did finally muster the courage to glance at her... he saw her looking at him differently. Differently to usual.

A wide-eyed stare.

"Come on," he said, turning around and walking towards those school doors. "We've... we've come this far. We do what we're here to do. We find this Nisha. And then we... and then we do whatever we have to do."

He looked at her again. She stayed staring at him. Eyes firmly focused on him.

He nodded at her.

And then he turned around, and he pushed the doors to the school's main entrance, and together, they stepped into the abyss...

NISHA

* * *

Nisha felt the hands grab her arms and push her towards Mrs Halloway's front door and she knew she was finished.

And then—and then she fell forward. She felt herself falling forward. Hitting the floor. Smacking her face against something hard. The ground. The concrete of the pavement. The...

No. Wait. It wasn't the concrete. It wasn't the hard ground. It was—it was something slightly softer. It was... carpet. She'd hit carpet. And she'd fallen forward and hit the carpet which meant...

The door.

Mrs Halloway's front door.

It was open.

She looked up. Saw Mrs Halloway standing there. She was old, and she always had rollers in her hair, which made her look like a weird alien and sometimes scared Nisha when she was just a little kid. Her house always smelled weird and sour. Dad used to say it was "musty" and that sometimes old people's houses smelled that way. Nisha wondered why that was. Why should old people smell any different to young people? Was it because the old was coming out of their skin? Was it because they were dying slowly, and that's what it smelled like when someone was dying slowly?

She was... she was standing over her. And she was pushing the door shut. And then—and then she was waving at Nisha. Pointing —pointing to the back of the house. Run. That's what she was telling her. Get away from here and run.

She looked up at Mrs Halloway standing at the door. She saw the hands of the bad people shooting through the gap in the door. Grabbing her. She saw their nails digging into her skin. Scratching at her. She wanted to help her. She wanted to stand between them. She wanted to stop them biting her, and she wanted to help her get away. Because she was always so nice to her. Always so kind to her.

But...

Dad.

Dad lived next door. If she could run out the back of the house, she could jump over the fence. She could sneak in through the back door. She could find him. He—he had to be there. He had to be.

Because if he wasn't... then where was he? He was working today maybe? But where? The hospital? Town? Where was he working?

She saw Mrs Halloway standing there. Struggling to hold the door shut. She shook her head, as tears stung her eyes.

"Go," Mrs Halloway mouthed. "Go!"

And as much as Nisha wanted to help, she turned around and she ran.

She ran down the hallway. Almost tripped on the rug in the hall. She saw Mrs Halloway's pictures all over the walls, all over the cabinets. Pictures of cats. Pictures of so many cats. She always had pictures of so many cats. And yet she didn't even *have* any cats. It didn't add up. It didn't make sense.

She ran towards the kitchen. It was the same layout as home, so she knew exactly where she was going. Down the hallway. Through the back door. She was going to get out of here. She was going to be okay. She was—

Movement.

Right in front of her.

Racing through the kitchen door. Three of them. The bad people. All running towards her.

She turned around and went to run back down the hallway when she saw Mrs Kirkham.

They were biting her. Biting her shoulder, one of them. A man. A man, wrapping his head around the side of the door. Sinking his teeth in. Blood oozing down her body, down her arm, and her mouth wide, like she was screaming.

And then that biter looked up, right into Nisha's eyes, and pushed the door open.

She looked over her shoulder. Looked at the three of them in the kitchen, running her way.

Then she turned around and saw that man banging and smacking the door, trying to push Mrs Halloway out of the way, and she felt—she felt trapped. She was trapped. She was trapped and she wanted Dad. She was trapped and she wanted...

Dwayne.

She thought about Dwayne, out there. Pictured him running in here. Pictured him running in here and—and saving her. Running in here and saving her and helping her and—and everything was going to be okay. Everything was going to be...

No.

She couldn't rely on him to save her.

And she couldn't think about the way they *hadn't* bitten her at school, or at the house, too much.

They were after her.

Which meant she needed to run.

She needed to hide.

She needed to get away.

She ran. Ran down the hallway. Ran towards the staircase. And the man at the door pushed Mrs Halloway away, pushed her away like she was nothing, like she was nothing at all, and Nisha knew she needed to get in one of the other rooms, she needed to...

The stairs.

She turned around. Ran up the stairs. She could barely move. She was frozen. Her legs were tingling and aching and she felt like she was running in mud. She ran over the stairlift, climbed over it, felt it start moving. She couldn't look back. She couldn't turn around. She couldn't—

She turned around. Turned around without even realising.

And then she saw them. Right behind her. Three, four of them, all scrambling up the stairs, all covered in blood, all splashing blood everywhere, their hands pressing against the banisters.

She turned around and she ran to the top of the stairs. She didn't know where to go. She didn't know where to hide. She just —she just knew she needed to get out of here. She needed to get next door, to Dad's. She needed to get away before they caught her. Before they hurt her. Before...

A tension. Right around her left ankle.

She tumbled over. Stumbled forward. And then she pictured the pain. She pictured them all sinking their teeth into her, all the bad people. She pictured them all biting her then she pictured herself turning into one of the bad people. But she wouldn't let herself turn into a bad person. She was good. Dad always taught her to be good. And she was going to stay good. She was always going to stay good.

She kicked back. And then she crawled and then ran further up the stairs. And then when she got to the top, she—she didn't know which way to turn. She didn't know which way to go. So instinctively, she ran into the bathroom. She turned around. Went to slam the door shut, when she saw them.

The bad people.

Racing towards the door.

So close.

So, so close.

She swung the door shut.

One of their hands stuck between the door and the frame.

She pulled it back. And even though she didn't want to hurt anyone, even though she didn't want to cause any pain, she pulled it back and she slammed it against that hand.

Hard.

But the hand wasn't moving.

She pressed herself against the door. She tried to reach for the lock. If she could just lock it, she could—she could get enough time to figure out what she was going to do.

She looked at that hand. Twisting. Shaking. Like a fish out of water.

And then she reached up for it.

She reached up for it and she smacked it.

Hard.

The hand disappeared behind the door.

The door slammed shut.

Nisha reached up for the lock with her shaking, twitching fingers. She slid it shut.

And then she backed off, away from the door, heart racing, breathing fast.

The door rattled on its hinges. They were out there. They were out there and they were trying to break in. They were out there and they were going to keep on trying to get in.

She stood there, shaking. Feeling sick. And then she took a deep breath, like Dad always told her to.

She turned around. Looked at the window, right above the toilet.

It was tiny.

She reached up for it. Tried to turn the handle. But—but it didn't budge.

She looked around for something she could use. Something heavy she could crack the glass with.

But the more she looked, the more she realised the truth.

She turned around.

Watched the door shake, and shake, and shake.

She wasn't getting out of this bathroom.

She wasn't finding Dad.

She was trapped.

And nobody was here to help her.

PETE

* * *

Pete felt the hands grab him and drag him back and for a moment, for just a moment, he thought he might just shit himself.

He watched her running away. Helen. Running into the distance. She'd—she'd pushed him. She'd pushed him and it wasn't a mistake. It wasn't a mistake at all. She'd intended to push him. She'd *wanted* to push him.

And now...

He heard shouting beside him. Snarling. Guttural cries and moans. Fingernails dug into his shoulders. He could hear teeth snapping, right by his ears, so close to biting him, so close to sinking into him. Maybe some of those fingernails were teeth. Maybe they were already sinking into him. Maybe they were already biting him and maybe his number was already up and...

No. No, he wasn't dying here. He wasn't a die-er. He was a fighter. And that's what he was going to do. Fight his way out of this.

He tried to drag himself away from that mass of hands. But

they just pulled him back. Dragged him further into the bushes. Dragged him closer towards those snapping jaws.

He watched Helen running away. Running as fast as she could. Bitch. That absolute bitch. He'd tried to save her. He'd—he'd pushed her through that bush and he'd saved her. And how had she thanked him? By pushing him into the bush. By serving him a death sentence.

He gritted his teeth and he lurched forward even more. He dug his heels in. He tried to stagger forward. Tried to pull himself free of those hands, grabbing him, holding him. But they kept on holding on. They kept on grabbing him. They kept on dragging him back.

But...

He wasn't letting Helen go.

He wasn't letting her run away.

No way. Not after what she'd done.

He sunk his feet further into the ground and suddenly, he tumbled forward.

He hit the grass. Face first. A tingling, stinging sensation split across his nose and his teeth. It took him back to childhood. Climbing over that stile with Granddad. Granddad lifting him over it, then slipping up, falling on top of him, and that burst of pain filling Pete's face, growing more and more painful. That realisation of pain. That first realisation of what pain really, truly was —and how everyone was susceptible to it.

And then he heard a cry right over his shoulder and then felt hands on his back and...

He rolled around. It was one of the kids. He couldn't remember the little prick's name, but he was a lot bigger than Pete remembered. Never a fat kid. Always a skinny little thing. Certainly piled on the pounds since Pete was forced to move out of his own home.

He pushed the kid back. The kid kept on trying to reach him, letting out this deep series of gasps. Blood oozed out of his fat lips. His skin glowed pale, like a ghost, almost purple actually. The veins on his temple bulged. And... and Pete realised something. His heart. This guy's heart was thumping like mad. Which meant... he was still conscious? He was still *alive* in there? Fuck. What was he even thinking? Of course he was still alive in there. These people, these infected, they weren't *zombies*. They weren't *dead*. They were... they were infected. Infected with some kind of sickness. Some kind of... rage.

He pulled back his fist and he punched the boy, square in the face.

The boy snapped at his knuckles. Behind, his mum, Carla, the most sour-faced prick Pete had ever met, scrambled to get through that hedge. Gasping. Snarling. And when he punched her kid, there was almost a look in her eyes of disapproval. Of protectiveness.

Was she still seeing this?

Was she still inside there, and witnessing this, like images on a screen?

He saw the fat kid above him. Saw him lunge towards him, move in for another bite. And Pete didn't have time to speculate. He didn't have time to get sentimental. He didn't have time to think.

He pulled his fist back further, and he cracked the kid right across the face.

He snarled. But the noise his mother made. That damned noise. He almost felt sorry for her. If she wasn't trying to kill him.

He pushed the fat kid off him. And then he staggered back. And then he looked down at this kid, crouched there on the ground. And in that moment of self-preservation—and that moment of total, bitter anger—Pete pulled back his foot and he buried it into the kid's skull.

He was surprised how easy it was to crack his skull. When he'd finished, when it was just twitching mush on the grass, he turned around, looked over towards where Helen had disappeared, and he tensed his fists.

He didn't know what he was going to do when he found her. Especially after this latest betrayal.

But he *was* going to find her.

He took another deep, shaky breath, and then he ran off into the distance.

And as he ran, he couldn't shake that feeling that Carla was watching him from behind those bloodshot, enraged eyes, screaming at his every move, as her boy lay twitching on the grass.

KEIRA

* * *

Keira had a bad feeling the second she stepped through the school doors.

The reception area was quiet, empty. A coffee cup sat on the desk, still steaming. Looked like whoever was here had just got up and left. And Keira felt torn. Torn between rushing through this school, racing to that Year Six classroom, and taking it slowly. Being careful. Because she just didn't know what might be hiding around every corner.

She turned around to the double doors in front of her. Took a deep breath, and walked over to them. And then she felt a hand. A hand, on her arm. She looked down. Saw Dad's hand. Holding her arm. She looked up at him, right into his eyes. He stared at her, with wide eyes.

"We need to be careful," he said.

Keira's face flushed. She pulled her hand away. Didn't need him protecting her. Didn't need him holding her like that. Even though... even though a part of her wanted to open up to him. Even though a part of her wanted to be honest with him. And even though a part of her *wanted* to forgive him. Now... now wasn't the time. And now wasn't the place.

She turned around. Looked at those dark brown double doors. Visualised the horrors that might await behind them. Children. A mass of infected children. Or—or emptiness. Just as terrifying.

Because if this place was empty, then it meant... Nisha was gone.

If this place was empty, she had no idea where else she had to go.

A knot tightened in her stomach, tighter and tighter. She took another deep breath. No more time to delay. No more time to hold back.

She walked towards those doors.

Pressed her hand against it. Felt the cool wood against her fingers.

She swallowed another lump in her throat.

And then she pushed the door open.

The door creaked as she pressed it. An echo, screeching through the school, made her hairs stand right on end. That screech, it was loud. It could draw attention right towards her. It could draw someone here. It could...

A hall stood in front of her. Tables covered the dark wood floor. Dinner tables, by the looks of things. There was a foody smell in the air. Something salty, something... something she couldn't really identify. Classic school mush. It took her right back. Right back to school dinners, as a kid. Sitting there with her packed lunch, watching the other kids eat their school dinners, and really wishing she could join them instead of her healthy sandwiches that Mum always forced her to eat. What she'd give for one of Mum's healthy sandwiches now.

But other than the tables, which had been partly laid out, and other than the food, cooking at the far side of the hall... it was pretty clear that this place was empty.

She took a deep breath and walked across the hall, towards

the doors on the other side of the hall. She could see a sign above those doors. JUNIORS. That's where she needed to be. That's where she needed to go. That's where Nisha would be—if she was anywhere.

"If we don't find her..." Dad started.

"We'll find her."

"We have to prepare ourselves. If we don't find her. It doesn't mean... it doesn't mean we've failed. Okay?"

She heard those words and she stopped. Right in front of the door to the junior side of the school. A knot, tightening in her throat. *It doesn't mean we've failed.*

"No," Keira said. "It means *I've* failed."

"You've risked everything to save a girl you've never met," Dad said. "If that's failure, then I'll be damned."

She looked around at him. Saw him half-smiling at her. And she smiled back at him. She had to. She couldn't help it. She felt... she felt pity for him. She could see how hard he was trying. How damned hard he was trying. And she could see how haunted his eyes looked. She could see the guilt, etched all over his face. He was trying. He really was trying.

And then she turned around. Not now. Now wasn't the time. Now wasn't the place.

She took a deep breath.

And then she lifted her hand and she pushed the next set of double doors open.

The second she opened these doors, Keira saw something in the corridor that made the hairs on the back of her neck stand on end.

Something... out of place with this school.

But something *inevitable*, somehow.

Blood.

Blood, right in the middle of the slightly off-white tiles in the corridor ahead of her.

She stood there. Frozen. A shiver rushed down her spine. She tasted sick, and she felt dizzy. She'd been sheltered from the horrors of outside for a good few minutes, or however long she'd been in here. And even though an empty school was creepy as hell, it was still a respite from the panic and horror outside.

She stared at this patch of blood. And then she felt a hand on her back. There for just a second. And reassuring for just a second, too. Dad. She looked at him. Then she looked back ahead, back down the corridor. And then she took another deep breath, and she walked.

Every single step she took, she looked from left to right, and over her shoulder. That blood. She couldn't escape that blood. What it meant. Trouble. Trouble, within the walls of this school. Violence, within the walls of this school. Horror, within the walls of this school.

Happy pictures surrounded her. Colourful pictures of rainbows, and hand-drawn animals, and silly cartoons. A happy place. A cheery place. But there was an artificiality about it. Empty schools were always creepy. She sneaked into school with a friend, Rose, back when she was a kid, and it just creeped her out. It felt... dead. Made her realise that it was the kids that gave schools life. That without the kids, school wasn't some magical place. It was just another building, but one with pretty pictures on the walls.

She had to keep focused. She had to keep moving. And she had to *listen*. Listen, at all times.

Because that blood on the floor meant someone was in here. Someone bad.

She had to be careful. So careful.

A sign caught her eye. Year Six. An arrow, pointing to the right. Her heartbeat picked up. Yes. Nisha's classroom. She—she just had to get to Nisha's classroom. She—she might be there. She might be in that classroom, hiding, waiting patiently. Even though the school was so quiet, even though the school was so empty, and even though blood smeared the floors... she might be in here.

She had to hope.

She had to believe.

She took another couple of steps when she saw something on her left.

Year Two. The Year Two classroom. The door was ajar. And she wasn't even sure why it caught her attention. Something about it just... just caught her eye. Even though she needed to focus. Even though she needed to focus on finding Nisha, on getting to that Year Six classroom, there was something about the Year Two room that caught her eye.

No. She couldn't get distracted. She couldn't let her focus wander. She turned around and walked down the corridor, around the corner, towards that Year Six room. Rufus whined behind her. His nails tapped on the hard floor. Dad was... quiet. Watching. Looking around, constantly scanning his surroundings.

She took a deep breath. Focused on that Year Six class entrance. Her heart raced. Heat filled her face. Through that door. Through that door and then—and then find Nisha. Find Nisha, and then...

Shit. What was she on about? Why was she kidding herself? What made her think Nisha would be here at all, when there was clearly nobody here?

She reached for the door. She grabbed the handle. She closed her burning eyes, and she swallowed a lump in her throat.

If we don't find her... it doesn't mean we've failed.

And then she turned the handle and she opened the door.

The Year Six classroom was like any classroom. Tables. Pens and pencils. Workbooks. More of those happy, smiley drawings on the wall. A whiteboard, with... with something etched on it. Smudged. Impossible to read.

But like the rest of the school, this classroom was empty.

Keira stepped into the classroom. She searched the workbooks. Harry Field. Lucinda Dwyer. All these names. All these little drawings and doodles, on every book.

"Keira," Dad said.

"I need to find her book."

"But we won't gain anything. Keira. I think—I think I hear..."

But she didn't hear what he was saying. Didn't hear anything. All his words, they just turned into noise. White noise.

She moved from table to table. From workbook to workbook.

Rasheed Patel.

Harriet Watson.

Louis... she couldn't read his surname. Terrible handwriting.

But she moved from table to table.

She had to find Nisha's book.

She had to find it, and she had to hope.

Rufus barked. "Rufus!" Dad gasped. And she could hear something now. Keira could hear something. Movement. Shuffling. Shuffling, somewhere in the heart of the school. Or was that in her imagination? Was that in her head? She didn't know. She didn't have a clue.

She just knew she needed to find Nisha's workbook.

She just had this intense feeling that if she found Nisha's workbook, she found a way out of here.

She searched every inch of the classroom, but none of the books were Nisha's.

Her stomach sank. Her heart raced. Something was wrong. Nisha, she was in Year Six. She was sure of it.

But if she was in Year Six... where was her book?

She looked up, over towards the teacher's desk. Ran over to it.

"Keira," Dad said, closing the door, gently. His eyes were wide. He looked... scared. "We need to hurry."

She ignored him. Ran over to the desk. She searched for the register. Then she grabbed it with her shaking hands. Dropped it. And then picked it up, letters tumbling out all over the floor.

A growl.

A growl, somewhere from the depths of the school.

And then a screech.

And then a cry.

She looked around. Over at Dad. At Rufus, growling beside him.

"Keira," Dad said.

She looked down at the register. Turned the pages. The notes, all scribbles. She couldn't read them. She couldn't see what they said. She couldn't process any of it. Just... just the name. Miss Ingrid.

And the list of students.

And then...

Nisha.

A light ignited inside Keira's chest.

Nisha.

She was here.

She was here, which meant—which meant she was right. This was the right classroom. This was the right place.

Which meant...

And then she saw something.

Right beside Nisha's name, she saw something that made her stomach sink.

"Keira!" Dad shouted. More growls. More screams. Echoing from outside the classroom. And getting closer.

But Keira couldn't say a word.

She could only stare at the words in front of her.

Those words, glaring back at her, like scribbles from a nightmare.

No longer a pupil.

She read those words again. Read them, as her heart beat faster. As her stomach sank to new depths. And as her eyes grew heavier, as her vision grew blurrier, the reality of what'd happened started to build up, started to grow, inside her mind.

The uniform, at home.

The work bag, at home.

"She doesn't... she doesn't come to this school anymore," Keira said.

She looked up. Looked over at Dad when she said it. And for a moment, for just a moment, she saw his eyes widen. She saw him open his mouth, as if he was going to say something. As if he didn't understand what she was saying. What she was getting at.

And then before he could say a word, the door behind him slammed open, and the windows on the right smashed open, and a group of snarling, screaming infected swarmed into the classroom from either side.

DWAYNE

* * *

T he moment Dwayne stepped through the doors of the Sunnydale Community Care Home, he knew there was something wrong.

It was silent. There was nobody at reception. The place reeked like it always reeked: a mixture of overpowering disinfectant and sour mustiness that always accompanied the old people in this place. The entrance area was usually so busy and bustling. A phone, constantly ringing. The grating chatter of the women behind the desk, who smiled and laughed with each other, but secretly threw daggers at each other.

But they weren't here anymore.

Dwayne swallowed a lump in his throat. He walked towards the door leading down towards the ward. To his left, behind the desk, he noticed one of the chairs was on its side. A cup of tea or coffee lay beside it, smashed. So the people here had fled in a hurry. A real hurry.

He gulped again. Walked over to the door. It was so silent in here. He couldn't hear anything at all. Had they already left? Had they already taken the residents out of this place? Had the police or the military dropped in and helped?

Or...

No. They wouldn't just *leave* them here, would they?

He grabbed the handle. Lowered it.

The second he opened the door, he got a horrid sour whiff— piss, shit, and old skin. But there was something else in the air, too. Something hanging there. Something unfamiliar. Almost... earthy. And almost...

Bloody.

He took a deep breath. Walked down the corridor, slowly. He didn't want to move too quickly. He had to be careful. Some- thing... something was wrong in this place. It was never a *nice* place by any stretch of the imagination. Exactly why he wanted to get Mum out of here, both before and after this outbreak of what- ever spread across the city.

But right now... right now, it felt creepier than usual. It felt even more ominous than usual.

He remembered the day he'd brought Mum here. He remem- bered the look of fear in her eyes, as he walked her down the corridor. How tight she held on to his hand, as he reassured her not to worry, that he wasn't going to leave her, that everything was going to be okay. And even though it broke him, even though he went home throwing his guts up, even though he cried the night away... he meant it. He truly meant it. He wasn't going to leave her in that place. He wasn't going to let her final months or years be trapped in that care home. He was going to get her out of there. And he was going to make sure she ended up some place nicer. Maybe even with him.

And that's why... that's why he'd turned back to a life of crime. He knew it'd make Mum mad, if she found out. He was on holiday in Spain with her and Cindy, his girlfriend at the time, a few years back. He was struggling to pay for stuff, and Mum kept on handing him cash, which embarrassed him awfully. She told him not to take it as an insult. But to treat Cindy. She liked Cindy. To keep her around. But also not to do anything stupid, for cash. That he had so much potential. That he was so much better than the petty crime he'd involved himself in ever since he finished school with no prospects.

He wished he could rewind to that moment. He wished he could've got home off that holiday and gone back to school, studied for a trade. But the easy money had been just too tempting for him. The drugs money. The robberies. The...

He cleared his throat, and he focused on the door at the end of the corridor. Right at the bottom.

Mum's room.

He took another deep breath. Picked up his pace. He looked through the little windows, passing all the rooms. Empty. No one here. So they'd taken them? They'd gone?

But...

He felt torn. If they'd taken them, then at least that meant Mum was out of here. But at the same time... where had they taken her? Phones were still out. There was no way of finding where they'd gone to.

And the more this nightmarish day progressed, the more Dwayne wondered whether things were ever going to get back to normal at all, ever again.

Where were the police? Where were the military? Where was the help?

He shook his head. Walked further down the corridor. Looked through more of those windows. Unmade beds. Television sets, flickering with white noise. Photographs laid across one of the beds, all in black and white, all ancient. Relics of the past.

He turned back to the bottom of the corridor, back towards Mum's room, when he noticed something.

There was... something on the door. Something written on the door. Something he couldn't see from here. A note. A note, etched in thick black ink.

He walked closer towards that door. A knot tightening in his stomach. What did that note say? And why was it written on Mum's door? Why was there something written on Mum's door, but not anyone else's?

A bang echoed somewhere behind him. Something tumbling over, hitting the floor. He looked around, over his shoulder. No sign of movement. Nothing.

He took a deep breath. Turned back around. And then he walked further down the corridor. Closer to Mum's room. Closer to that writing. Closer to...

The writing.

He could read it now.

But the more he read it... the less he understood.

STAY AWAY.

His heart started beating faster. Stay away? What did it mean? Stay away from who? Stay away from...

And then he saw the blood.

The speckles of blood, all over the window of Mum's room.

He stepped towards it, his stomach knotting, his body tensing up. "Mum," he gasped. He needed to get in that room. He needed to know she was okay. He needed...

A bang.

The door, to Mum's room, rattling on its hinges.

A face appeared. Right at the glass.

Dwayne's body froze. His stomach sank. Because—because that face. He knew that face. He knew it so well.

It was Mum.

Only...

Mum's eyes were vacant. Red. Bloodshot. She scratched the glass. Tried to bite it with her snapping jaws.

And between those teeth, which were surprisingly good for a woman of her age... blood.

Dwayne's eyes clouded up. A cloud surrounded him. He lost

all sense of where he was. Of *who* he was. And all he saw was... all he saw was Mum.

Mum.

The anger in her eyes.

The blood between her teeth.

And that horrible snarl, from her throat.

Mum was here.

But Mum... Mum *wasn't* here.

She wasn't here at all.

He was too late.

Mum was already infected.

Mum was already gone.

HELEN

Helen hadn't been running long when she got the horrible sense that she was being followed.

It started when she reached the vets, right beside her house. Just this feeling. This instinctive sense that someone was watching her. That someone was behind her. That someone was chasing her. And it made sense. She'd heard the reports of the attacks. And, fuck, she'd *seen* it with her own damned eyes.

But it wasn't just these infected people she was worried about.

It was Pete.

She looked over her shoulder, back down the road. She looked at the long, country lane, stretching off into the distance. She saw the hills, overlooking her house, so beautiful, so gracious. Maybe she could disappear up there. Maybe she could hide in the wilderness until all this blew over.

Billy.

Pete.

Billy, lying dead on the living room floor.

And Pete...

She didn't know what possessed her to push him into that family of infected. Part hatred for the years of torment he'd caused her, however unwittingly. Part anger at him, for—for killing Billy.

Billy.

Billy was dead.

Billy was dead and John was bitten and Carla was—was infected and her kids were infected and...

She collapsed. She collapsed to the road. She—she couldn't breathe. She felt like she'd been kicked in the stomach. Shit. She had to keep going. She had to keep moving. But how could she keep moving when the world wouldn't stop spinning? And how could she keep moving when she knew what she'd done?

The world spun around her as she crawled along the road. Not even thinking, as the gravel dug into her bare knees. Just—just trying to get home. Home. She needed home. That's what she needed more than anything else right now. Home. Go home. Go to bed. Or—or go into the bathroom and lock the doors and run a long bath and just—just wait. Just wait, and pretend everything is okay, pretend Billy is still alive, pretend everything is...

And then she saw it.

Up the road. Right up ahead.

People.

Four of them. Four that she could see, anyway.

All running down that road.

All running towards her.

Her stomach sank. She smelled wee, and she felt a dampness around her groin. She had to be strong. She had to stand up and she had to be strong. She had to stand up and be strong. She could do this. She had to do this.

She stood. Her knees wobbled. Her legs tingled. And she looked at the building to the left of her—the little outhouse, she didn't even know what it was, some sort of brick building that apparently linked up with the old bunker near the back of hers.

Pete always said he was going to go in there and explore it one day. Billy, too. But neither of them did. Neither of them went in there. Neither of them investigated it.

And neither of them would ever get the chance to.

But now she would.

She had to.

She limped towards that outhouse. She reached the gate, pushed it, but it wouldn't open. It was blocked. She tried to lift her leg, tried to climb over it, but her leg was just so heavy, and her body was so weak, and—

Screaming.

Down the road.

Getting closer.

And more of them, too.

She turned around. She closed her eyes. She took a deep breath of that warm summer air.

"You've got this," she gasped. "You've got this."

She lifted her heavy foot. She climbed over the gate, pulling herself over it. And then she dropped over the other side. Collapsed in a heap. And she was so tempted to just stay there. Stay there and let them catch up with her. Stay there and—and hope they made it quick. Stay there and hope she didn't turn into whatever they were.

But no.

She wasn't dying.

Not today.

She pushed herself up. Pushed herself up with her weak, shaking arms. She had to get up. She had to get the hell up and she had to get to that building before they got to her. She had— she had to break inside it. She had to break inside it and she had to close those doors and she had to hide.

She heard more screaming. Even closer now. More growling and shouting, even louder.

"Come on, Helen," she said, picturing her dad, imagining what he'd say to her. "Get up. Get the fuck up."

And then, she took another deep breath, and she stood.

She staggered over to the door of the outbuilding. She ran around the side of it, as the footsteps and screaming grew closer. She had to break the lock. She looked around for a rock. For something she could use to smash it up with. It might be a long shot, but she was going to try. She wasn't giving up.

She ran around the side of the outbuilding when she noticed something odd.

The door.

The door was partly open.

The lock lay smashed by its entrance.

A shiver crept down Helen's spine. If the door was open and the lock was broken, did that mean... someone was in there?

She heard more growls. Heard more snarls. Infected. Infected, banging at the gate. Trying to clamber over.

Helen turned to the door. Heart racing. Sweat pouring down her face.

And as much as she didn't want to go through that door, as much as the darkness and the unknown terrified her... she knew she didn't have a choice.

She squeezed in through that small gap.

And then she pulled the door shut as hard as she could.

Darkness surrounded her.

She stepped back. Covered her mouth with her hands. Shaking. Panting. She'd—she'd done it. She'd escaped. But—but now she had to be quiet. Now she had to be quiet. She had to wait. She had to wait for a moment. She had to wait for an opportunity. She had to wait for a chance. And then she had to—

Out of nowhere, a pair of hands grabbed her, and wrapped around her mouth.

She tried to scream, but those hands pressed so hard against her lips that she couldn't open her mouth.

And then she heard a voice.

A voice that sent a shiver, right down her spine.

An impossible voice.

But a voice she couldn't deny.

"Ssh," Pete said. "It's okay. I've got you. You're safe now. We're both safe now."

DAVID

* * *

David felt the door swing open and knock him to the floor, and he knew he was in deep, deep shit.

He could hear screaming. Everywhere. A window smashed somewhere up ahead. Footsteps echoed right behind him, as snarls filled the classroom. The infected. They were here. They were here in this classroom and—and he needed to get away. He needed to get out. And he needed to get Keira out of here, too.

He looked up. Saw Keira standing there, holding onto this register. Her eyes were wide. Beside him, he could hear Rufus barking, standing his ground, kicking his back paws back. No. No, he couldn't stay here. He couldn't stand his ground. He had to run. He had to go. He had to go, right this second.

But still he stayed there.

Still, he barked.

David looked up. Two of those infected, clawing through the window, grunting, groaning. Two men. Both dripping blood. Dressed in suits. Teachers, by the looks of things.

And then...

He saw more of them.

More of them. Outside. And suddenly it hit him. Suddenly it dawned on him. The playground. They—they were coming from the playground. They'd got out of here, and now they were breaking back in, and—

A hand. A hand around his ankle. Tight. Digging right into his flesh.

He swung around. Saw a kid. Tall. Skinny. Blonde hair and bright blue eyes. Covered in blood. Tooth marks across his throat. Anger in his dead eyes.

David kicked him, tried to get him off. Felt bad about kicking a kid. Really bad. But he didn't have a choice. He didn't have a choice at all. He needed to get him off. He needed to get out of this classroom. And he needed to get Keira out of it with him. Keira and Rufus.

He kicked the kid back, but he kept on gripping on to David's ankle. Shit. Stubborn little bastard. And all the time, beside him, Rufus barked. Haunting shouts and yelps echoed through the classroom. More windows smashed, and more of them got inside. They were running out of time.

He dragged the kid away from the door. Saw two more of them, running inside. But none of them beyond that. Just... just an empty corridor. And a door. A door leading out the front of the school. A chance. A chance to get away. A chance to escape.

He looked around. Saw Keira wrestling with one of them. A man. Way bigger than her. Shit. He needed to get up. He needed to help her.

He looked up at the kid and he felt so sorry for him. For what he'd been through to put him in this state.

But then he had to switch that sympathy off. He had to switch it right off.

He pulled back his fist and he cracked him, square in the nose.

And then he stood up. He ran. He ran over to Keira. Ran over to her, wrestled the man holding her away from her. Grabbed him around the waist, and threw him to the ground.

And then he grabbed Keira. Held her arms.

"We go," he said. "Now. Okay? Now."

She looked him in the eyes with those tearful eyes of her own, and she nodded.

"Now," she said. "N..."

Another smash. A window, right across the room, smashing to pieces. Eight of them in here. Eight of them that he could see.

He looked around the classroom. He saw the eight infected. And he saw more of them. So many of them. Hours into this outbreak and there were already so many infected. So many of them.

And then he looked at the doorway.

An opening.

An opportunity.

A chance.

He saw that opening and he felt a knot in his chest.

He was at that car again. He was on the road again. He was staring at Rina, and at Keira, inside that car. And he was frozen. He couldn't move. He couldn't help them. He couldn't save them.

Only...

He grabbed Keira.

He turned her around.

He looked right into her eyes.

"You need to get out of here."

Keira opened her mouth. "What—"

A shout. From the doorway. More of them. Kids, now. Kids, covered in blood, running into this classroom. Blocking the door.

"The window," David said, pointing over to his right. "You have to go. You and Rufus. Right now."

Keira shook her head. "But—"

"There's no time," David said. "There's... there's no time. I'm sorry. I love you. And I always will."

And Keira stood there. She stood there, frozen. But no. She couldn't freeze. She couldn't freeze right now. Not right now.

"Go," David shouted.

"But—"

"Go!"

And then, as if in slow motion, Keira ran.

She ran towards the window.

She ran past the infected, who lunged at her.

She ran towards that smashed glass, and then she turned around and she looked back at him, Rufus by her side, wide-eyed.

He looked right at her. His eyes clouding up with tears. His vision blurring.

And then, amidst all the screaming, amidst all the horror, David smiled.

"I love you," he said. "I always did."

She opened her mouth. Like she was going to say something back to him.

And that's when he saw it.

At that instant, at that moment, he saw it, and everything stood still.

The infected.

Appearing at the broken window.

Grabbing Keira.

Dragging her towards him.

And then wrapping his teeth around her right forearm.

DWAYNE

* * *

Dwayne saw Mum pressed up against the glass of her room and he knew right away that she was gone.

She was pressed right up against the glass of the window. Her eyes were bloodshot. Tears streamed down her cheeks. Tears of blood. She scratched the glass with her long, uncut nails. Gnawed at it, slobbering all over it. And seeing her like this... seeing her like this was a gut punch. A total gut punch.

Because it meant he was too late.

And it meant Mum was already gone.

Seeing her here, alone in her room. Abandoned. The care home had been abandoned otherwise. And what dignity had Mum been shown? She'd been locked in her room. STAY AWAY, etched across the door. Left in here, frightened. Left in here, alone. And even though she was infected, even though Dwayne had no doubts that she wanted to kill him right now, just like Nico wanted to kill him, just like so many others today had wanted to kill him... he felt so, so sorry for her. Because this was Mum. And he loved Mum.

He reached for the handle with his shaking hand. Placed it there. Tears streamed down his cheeks. His heart raced. He felt— he felt pain. The same sort of pure pain he'd felt when he found Granddad sitting in his favourite chair. He always sat there, snoring away. Dwayne used to creep up to him. Cover his nostrils, making him gasp. He'd chase Dwayne around the house like a tiger, and when he caught him, the pair of them would play fight and laugh for hours.

Only that one day... Granddad wasn't breathing. He didn't gasp. He didn't get up and chase Dwayne. He was gone.

He looked in through the glass at Mum. He watched her banging on the door. Such anger. Such pain. And—and it wasn't much dissimilar to when he'd last visited her. No, wait. The time before last. She was confused. She was angry. Started a fight with another resident, apparently. Restrained, for her own good.

Dwayne would never forget walking into her room and hearing the most awful words come out of her mouth. Not that the odd "fuck" or "shit" bothered him. But hearing those words come from *Mum's* mouth. It just seemed... wrong. So damned wrong. And so sad.

He stood at that door. Holding that handle. And a part of him wanted to just lower that handle and walk in that room with her. Let... let whatever happen, happen. Because everything he was doing. The robbery. The job. He was doing it so he could secure her a better life. He was going to get her out of here. And then he was going to fly to Spain. She was going to be safely cared for in a better place than this council-run shithole. And her final years were going to be comfortable. Not fearful. Not painful.

But she was gone.

He lowered the handle when a face flickered in his mind.

Nisha.

Nisha, running down that road.

Nisha, trying to avoid the infected.

And what had he done?

He'd walked away from her. He'd abandoned her. He'd left her. All because he wanted to find Mum.

And now here she was. Here Mum was.

It was already too late for Mum.

He let go of the handle, as Mum banged at the glass. He remembered the *last* time he'd come to see her. She was so much more peaceful. So much happier. So much more content. No swearing. And she knew who he was. Exactly who he was.

He remembered something she'd said to him. "You'd put me out of my misery if ever I was suffering, wouldn't you, honey?"

And he'd laughed it off. Told her to stop being daft. That she wasn't going to suffer. And of course he knew deep down he could never do that to her. He could never "put her out of her misery". He wasn't capable of it. He didn't have it in him.

But now, looking at her standing there, staring out at him... he saw her suffering. More than he'd ever seen her suffering. The rage in her eyes. The anger in her eyes. And the pity in her eyes. He knew what she would want right now. And he knew what he had to do for her.

He rolled down his sleeves.

He grabbed the handle.

And then he took a deep breath, blinked away his mass of tears, sniffed up, trying to stay calm, trying to keep his composure, and then he pushed the door against her, gently.

She pressed back. Pressed back as hard as she could. Snarled at him. Gasped at him.

"It's okay, Mum," he said. "It's—it's your Dwayne. It's me. Okay? It's me."

And really, as he pushed open the door, as he stepped inside this stuffy, smelly room, in a way this wasn't much different to his usual visits. The anger. The frustration. And having to explain who he was to her. It was just like his normal visits. That's what he had to tell himself. Just an ordinary visit.

He pushed harder against the door. Pushing her back, out of

the way, as she tried to grab him, as she tried to bite him, as she tried to reach him.

"It's okay," he said. Trying not to cry. "I'm—I'm here. I'm here."

He stopped. Stopped right there, Mum behind the door, trying to get to him. He saw the bed opposite. And he knew that was his best opportunity. He knew that was his best chance.

He closed his burning eyes, and he took a deep breath.

"I'm sorry," he said.

And then he pushed the door.

Hard.

He pushed the door so hard that Mum went tumbling back onto the bed, cracking her head on the bed head. She yelped in pain. And it was a yelp that made him think she was still in there. That whatever rage had come over her had passed, and she was just Mum again, she was okay, and he didn't have to do what he feared he was going to have to do.

But then he saw her jolt up. Bleeding from her head.

He heard that guttural gasp, directed at him.

And he knew what he had to do.

He ran over to her.

He pushed her down. Onto the bed. She grabbed his arms. Grabbed them tight. Like when he fell off the boat as a kid on that boat tour in Turkey, and she reached in and grabbed him so tight he thought his hands were going to fall off.

And then he dragged the pillow over towards her face.

He saw her. Saw her staring up at him. Spluttering blood. And just as he moved that pillow over her face, he thought he saw a glimmer of recognition in her eyes. A glimmer of recognition. A tear, tainted with blood.

And then he pressed the pillow over her face and pinned her down.

She punched him. She tried to scratch him. Blood seeped through the pillow. But he kept on holding it down. He kept on holding it down as she struggled, he kept on holding it down until her snarls turned into cries, desperate cries, and he kept on holding it down as her movement grew weaker, as her punches grew more flailing.

"It's okay, Mum," Dwayne said. Sobbing. "It's—it's okay."

He stared at that photo of him, Mum and Dad, on the beach, ice creams in hand, smiles on their faces.

"It's okay. It's okay."

He had no idea how long he held that blood-drenched pillow over her face.

But eventually, she stopped struggling.

Eventually, she stopped gasping.

Eventually... Mum finally stopped suffering.

PETE

* * *

Pete held Helen close and listened to the groans and the growls outside.

It was dark in this out house. It led down to an old military bunker right behind his house. Cold War bunker. Back in the day, it was supposed to be the place where important people from the North West all gathered if ever a nuke went off. Kind of reassuring, having a place like that behind his home.

But it wasn't what it used to be. The military sold it off to some farmer, and then it ended up being bought and renovated by some restaurant owner—gutted, and robbed of all its potential protective benefits. Shame. Might've come in handy in a time of crisis like today.

He could hear Helen whining under his grip. He could feel the warmth of her saliva against his hand. And he kept on seeing her, standing opposite him in the field. A chance to walk away together. Even after everything that'd happened, a chance to walk away...

And she pushed him.

Pushed him right into that crowd of infected.

And he was lucky. He was so lucky Farmer John's nut job family hadn't ripped him apart. And he could barely believe his luck that Helen had found her way to the same damned outhouse as he had. It almost felt like... like fate.

Some paths were just meant to cross, weren't they?

"Ssh," he said, holding her mouth tight. "It's me. Okay? It's me. Be quiet. Try not to make a noise. Don't want them to hear us, do we? It's okay. I've got you. It's okay."

He stayed really quiet. Really still. He didn't know how these infected people operated. On rage, sure, he knew that. But did they have a heightened sense of smell or anything? No. They just seemed to be... well, angrier people. Angrier people than the average person. Purely running on adrenaline. And their wounds. Some of their wounds looked... they looked unsurvivable. But somehow, they were surviving them. Would they burn out eventually? Die of blood loss? How did it work?

He listened to that chorus outside and he wondered whether they could be fooled. What differentiated an uninfected from one of their own.

He hoped he lived long enough to find out.

And then he heard it.

Banging.

Banging, right in front of him.

The door. There was one of them at the door. And try as he might, he couldn't close that door again. He could only pull it so far.

They were here.

They were here and they were going to find him. Somehow, they were going to find him, and Helen.

He turned Helen around in the darkness. Looked her, right in the eye. "Listen to me," he said, still holding her mouth. "There's a ladder at the back. It leads onto the roof. We can climb that.

Get on top. And then... and then, well, we'll have a better chance of getting away than we do in here."

She stared at him. Behind, the door rattled. More of them. Shit. More of them, gasping. Growling louder now. Alerting the others? That's what it sounded like. More of them. Dragging the door open, trying to open it, even though he'd wedged it shut. There were too many of them. They were going to break in here. They were going to get him. And they were going to get Helen.

And even though Helen had hurt him, even though she'd tried to *kill* him... he didn't want anything happening to his dear wife.

She was his.

"We're going to climb that ladder. Understand? We're going to climb that ladder and we're going to get out of here. Or we'll die in here. Understand?"

He kept his hand there. Kept it there a few seconds.

And then, when he was sure she was going to comply, he moved it away. Slowly. Gradually.

"We're going to—"

"I'd rather die right here than go anywhere with you. You fucking murderous, pathetic scumbag."

And then she spat right in his face.

Pete felt... like he'd been stabbed. And suddenly, the infected disappeared into the background. Suddenly *everything* disappeared into the background. And all he heard were Helen's words. Helen's painful, stabbing words.

"I wish I'd never met you," Helen said. "I wish I'd never married a pathetic weak fuck like you. And I wish you'd died when I'd pushed you into that bush. I wish John would've ripped you apart."

He heard these words, and the pain sunk in, deeper and deeper. Stinging him. Stinging him like nettles, all over his body.

The crying got louder.

The growling got louder.

The infected banged away at that door, louder and louder.

Helen stepped up to him. Right up to him. Squared up to him. Stared into his eyes.

"I wish you were dead," she said. "I never loved you. I pitied you. You're a weak, pathetic man. And every man I've ever been with has been way more of a man than you."

He felt his jaw tense.

He saw the door open up, right up.

He saw the light fill the outhouse.

He felt Helen rush towards him, rush towards those ladders.

And he stopped her.

He put a hand on her shoulder, and he stopped her.

"Very well," he said.

And then he pushed her back into the oncoming crowd of infected.

Hard.

He watched her fall into that crowd.

He watched her eyes widen.

He saw her mouth open. "Pete—Pete no Pete please Pete —ARGH!"

And then he saw them bite her throat.

He saw blood splatter out of her neck.

He saw a woman behind her bite her head, and another man pin her down and gnaw at her face, tearing the skin and the flesh away.

He watched her die, right before him. He listened to her screams.

And as the tears flowed down his face, he took a deep breath, turned around, and climbed up the ladder.

"I'm sorry, my love," he whimpered. "I'm sorry…"

DWAYNE

* * *

Dwayne stood outside the care home and listened to the sound of the birds singing.

It was pretty gorgeous, to be honest. The day so far had consisted of screams. Of the sound of his heart, thumping blood around his skull. Of the sound of cars, crashing into each other. Sirens wailing.

And of crying.

His own crying.

He stood there and he looked at the houses in the distance. At the smoke rising from afar. He could smell that smoke in the air, strong. Mixing with the scent of blood. The *taste* of blood, too. The taste of blood and sweat.

And in his memories, taunting him, Mum.

His stomach sank when he thought of Mum. He forgot the beauty of the birds. He forgot the momentary bliss he'd felt, at that moment where he just stood there, listened to nature, and let all the chaos and all the pain drift into the background.

And he felt the burning, stinging sensation in his eyes, as those tears continued to roll down his face.

Mum was gone. He'd... put her to rest. He'd put that pillow over her face and he'd felt her, struggling. He'd listened to her, screaming, almost begging underneath that pillow. But he'd held that pillow over her face and he'd done what she would've wanted him to do. Even though she was scared, even though she was afraid... she wasn't suffering anymore. The suffering was over.

When he pulled the pillow away, he half-expected her to shoot to her feet. To spark back to life, like a zombie or something. 'Cause that's what this infection felt like. A zombie outbreak.

But she'd suffocated. She'd died, right there. And as much as that taught him something about this infection—that these infected people still relied on the same motor functions as he did —he couldn't see it that way. He couldn't comprehend anything in normal terms right now.

All he could think about was Mum.

And how sorry he was for what he'd done to her.

He looked across the street. His vision blurry. His head spinning. His stomach aching. His knees shaking. And he felt... he felt lost. Today was supposed to be about stealing the money he needed to get his mum out of this shitty care home. Today was supposed to be about getting that plane to the Costa Del Sol and starting a new life. A new life, away from crime. A new life, away from all the sins of his past. A new beginning. For him, and for Mum.

But Mum was gone. And the money was gone. And somehow, with the state of affairs on the streets, he didn't get the feeling anyone was getting out of the country any time soon. Nobody wanted this virus spreading beyond these borders—if indeed they were confined to these borders. The COVID-19 wasn't a lockdown. Not really. *This* was a lockdown. You stepped outside your home, you died. And the speed with which this virus spread, the speed with which people seemed to turn into those infected... he didn't hold much hope for the survivors here.

He thought about the police. He could still hear sirens in the distance, less so, now. Some of them would have a plan. Some of them would create "safe zones", and try to instil a sense of order, while the nation found its feet again. And the military, even more so. He was surprised they hadn't stepped in already. Surprised they hadn't sent out some emergency broadcast beyond the initial "STAY AT HOME" command, before the news went black, before the networks became overloaded, before *everything* stopped working.

But that would come. In time, that would come. Dwayne was sure of it.

But Mum wasn't here for any of it.

He looked down the street and he thought about Nisha. The kid. The kid he'd been looking after. The kid he'd helped out of Pedo Harry's car. And the kid who'd... who'd *saved* him.

And if he hadn't saved her... would he have got to the care home in time to save Mum? Would things have turned out differently?

But... that didn't feel right, somehow. Thinking that way, it felt wrong.

Because make no mistake about it. There was something different about her. The way she'd stood there, in the kitchen. The way the infected raced towards her, then stopped, as if there was a brick wall between them. And the way she'd run down that street, mostly evading them, as she hurtled towards her home.

There was something different about Nisha.

And even if there *wasn't* anything different about Nisha... even if she was just an ordinary kid... Dwayne still felt this guilt. This guilt, for walking away from her. This guilt, for leaving her.

And this sense of... connection. This strange, inexplicable sense of connection. A sense of connection he couldn't explain. A sense of connection he didn't understand.

But a sense of connection that was undeniably *there*.

He took a deep breath of the humid summer air. Swallowed a sickly lump in his throat. He thought about Mum. What Mum would say, if she were still here now.

Go after her. Save her. She's important. And even if she's not important... she's important to you.

He closed his eyes. Swallowed another lump, as the tears dripped from the bottom of his chin. And as he stood there, in the midst of this sea of chaos, he felt himself bobbing along on a lifeboat of hope.

He tightened his fists.

He took a deep breath.

He was going to find Nisha.

And he was going to protect her.

No matter what it took.

He looked around. Looked back at the care home.

"I'm sorry, Mum," he said. "I... I love you. I'm sorry I couldn't save you. I'm sorry I couldn't have been there earlier. But I hope —I hope you're resting now."

And then he turned around, faced the road, and he walked back towards Nisha's home.

Somewhere overhead, he heard the distant sound of helicopter rotors, edging closer and closer...

NISHA

* * *

Nisha watched the bathroom door rattling on its hinges and waited for the bad people to burst inside.

The door rattled. Again and again and again. She could see shadows flickering underneath it. Their feet. And the shadows of their fingers, too, clutching at the sides of the door. The bathroom smelled sweet, like Grandma's bathroom used to smell. But there was another smell in the air, too. That weird smell that all the bad people smelled of. Like... like mud. Like mud on a warm, rainy day. She used to like that smell. She didn't anymore.

She gulped. Tasted something weird in her mouth. Something metal. Like blood. She thought about Mrs Halloway. Dragging her into her home. Being bitten. Being bitten, all over her body. That poor lady being bitten and being beaten up, right in front of her.

She looked over at the wall beside her. The bathroom wall. The bedroom, beside her. And then... and then the next wall, and then *her* bedroom. She was so close. So close to home. So close to her bedroom. So close to... to *Dad*. Because—because he was there somewhere. He was there and if she went into that house and into that bedroom, she'd find him, and if she didn't find him, he'd find her eventually. He'd come in there and he'd find her and everything would be okay. Everything would be okay.

But... but she looked back around at the door. Saw it shaking. She couldn't get out of that door. And she couldn't get through the wall. And she looked back at the window, too. It was too small. And—and she'd already tried it. It wouldn't budge. And there was nothing heavy in here she could use to smash it with either. Even if there was... it looked thick. And even if she could smash it... the drop down to the garden was really far. A kid called Holly a few doors down fell out when she was sleepwalking once. She broke her neck and died. It scared Nisha. She told Dad to lock her window and make sure he hid the keys. She didn't like the thought of sleepwalking and falling out the windows without even realising it.

She sat there. Shaking. She thought about the kitchen. How those bad people surrounded her, but how they didn't do anything. How they didn't attack her. And then she thought about Mrs Thompson. How she'd grabbed her. How she'd pinned her up against the wall. How she'd tried to bite her... and then how she'd dropped her. Let her go. She was—she was different. Even if those bad people broke the door down, they might not hurt her. She might be okay.

But... but she still wasn't sure.

And she didn't want to find out.

But what choice did she have?

She sat there. Sat there, shaking, against the sink. She thought of Dad. She thought of him coming in here. She thought of him holding her. Holding her and then the bad people breaking down the door and Nisha standing in his way and—and helping him. Saving him. Stopping them getting to him. And then they could go back home, together, and wait for the people on the telly who ran the country to get things back to normal, even though Dad always said he hated them.

She watched that rattling door and she thought of... of Dwayne. She'd run away from him. She shouldn't have run away from him. 'Cause—'cause he was right. The road was dangerous. The road wasn't safe. And she should've waited. She should've waited 'cause she hadn't found Dad anyway, so why bother? She'd found no one. She'd just got herself trapped. Got herself trapped in here. And there was no getting away. There was no way out.

She thought about Dwayne. Imagined the window smashing. Imagined him swinging in on a rope, and then grabbing her and swinging out with her, together. She imagined them both finding Dad. And all of them finding somewhere safe to live, together. Maybe Dwayne would find his mum, too. He wanted to find his mum. She hoped he did. He seemed like a nice person. She didn't know who he was or where he was from, but he seemed like a nice person, and she hoped he was okay.

She sat there in the bathroom. Sat there, alone. Sat there, and watched the door shaking, more and more. She closed her eyes. Squeezed them, tight. So tight that the darkness came, and then in the place of the darkness, colours. Colours, filling her vision. And if she sat like this long enough... she wouldn't even know. She wouldn't know when they broke in. She wouldn't know until they grabbed her, and even then they'd bite her, and it would be quick, and—and—

No.

No, she had to be strong.

She'd been strong before. She'd scared them away before. But —but she couldn't stop thinking of Ginger Harry, and Mrs Thompson, and she couldn't stop thinking of Beth, and—and all of it just made her breathing heavier, all of it just made her crying harder, all of it just made her...

Freeze.

She sat there. Sat there and imagined she was on a beach. Dad beside her. Warm sand between her toes. The cool water hitting her feet, tickling them. But it wasn't just Dad here. It was Dwayne, too. Dwayne, and his mum. And Beth. Her friends. The best friends she had.

She sat there in the darkness, and felt a warm tear roll down her face.

She was going to be okay.

She was strong.

She was...

She opened her eyes, and she saw it, right in front of her.

The lock, snapping away.

The door, swinging open.

And then the crowd of bad people, hurtling into the bathroom, and running right at her.

She closed her eyes and disappeared to the beach again.

She was okay.

She was safe.

She was...

PETE

* * *

Pete walked aimlessly down the road with no real goal in sight, and he wondered whether he had it in him to take his own life.

The skies were cloudy. Rain sprinkled down from above. Everything around him was in... in a haze. A distant haze. He could hear the same sirens, the same screams, in the distance. But they seemed... far away, somehow. The ringing in his ears. That haze he was under, surrounding him.

The haze of memories.

The haze of... of *her* screams.

Helen's screams.

And what he'd done to her.

He thought back to the sound she made when he pushed her into that crowd of infected people. The scream, blood-curdling. And it was like... it was almost like he didn't actually realise what he'd done until he heard that scream. He wanted to jump in there with her. He wanted to *die* with her. Die beside her. That was always his goal. That was always his plan. In sickness and in health. Well, in *death* too.

But he was too afraid. He was too fucking cowardly to kill himself.

And besides... why *should* he?

Helen tried to kill him. Several times.

She'd ruined his life. And then she'd tried to kill him. So really, he'd just done what anyone would've done, right? Maybe—maybe he was a victim of abuse. He'd never really thought about it that way before, but maybe that's how it was. A victim of abuse. She'd abused him. Taken advantage of his better nature.

And he'd... he'd just *snapped*.

He wandered aimlessly down the road. He knew he was risking it. He knew an infected might just jump out at any moment. Attack him. Tear him to pieces. And even though he wasn't quite in touch with the reality of that possibility originally... now, he didn't want that.

He didn't want to die.

Why *should* he die?

He had no reason to die. He'd—he'd not done anything wrong, other than... Okay, maybe *killing* Billy was a bit extreme.

But Billy took everything from him. He took his wife from him. He took his *life* from him. So he could hardly blame himself. He'd—he'd snapped. That's what'd happened. He'd snapped, after so many years of being beaten down, so many years of being trodden down, and after so many years of feeling like he was worthless, useless... something snapped.

He stopped. Heard the sirens. Smelled the smoke. And suddenly, as he stood in the middle of this collapsing street, in a daze, it dawned on him that he was supposed to be at the forefront of the response to this type of situation. He was supposed to be a police officer. He was supposed to represent law, and order.

And what was he doing?

Wandering aimlessly through the streets?

No. No, that wasn't good enough. That wasn't good enough at all.

He needed to be better. He needed to be *stronger.* He needed to be who he was hired to be. He needed to fulfil his duty. His duty to his city. His duty to his people.

The radios might've gone out. The confusion might be just as rife at the station. They might not have any orders. But Pete was an officer of the law. An officer of law and order. And already, he was seeing evidence of looting. Of rioting. Of the situation spilling out of control, and not just with the infected, either.

He had no purpose as Pete anymore. He had no *life* as Pete anymore.

But he had a purpose as Detective Constable Pete.

This was his life now.

He stood there, in the middle of the road.

He took a deep breath.

And then he reached into his pocket, and pulled out his badge.

He slapped it on his chest. Gritted his teeth.

And then he walked off down the road.

He had work to do.

He had a street to take control of.

He looked around at the man walking off into the distance, completely alone.

Dwayne Rutherford. Real piece of shit. Criminal prick. Evaded the law for way too long. Went to prison, then spat right back out onto the streets to spread his shit, all over again. He'd punched Pete once. Said some really belittling stuff to him. Spat in his face. Real piece of work. And Pete never forgot. He never, ever forgot.

He looked over at him and he felt a bitter sense of satisfaction creeping up inside.

It was time to clean up the streets.

It was time to deal with the trash.

It was time to stop the city of Preston from imploding, once and for all.

KEIRA

* * *

Keira felt the hand grab her arm out of nowhere, and drag her towards the window.

Time stood still. The classroom faded around her. The happy, smiling faces pinned to the wall disappeared from view. And Dad. Dad, and Rufus, standing there. Dad glaring at her. Shouting at her. And Rufus. Rufus, barking at her from outside the broken window. All of it faded away. She couldn't hear what Dad was saying. She could barely even hear Rufus's barks anymore. And the screams, and the grunts, and the gasps, all of them filling the classroom... all of it faded into nothingness. The infected, so many in here, all of them paled into insignificance.

Because of that hand, on her arm.

She turned around and saw one of the infected holding on to her. A middle-aged man. Spiked grey hair. Stunk of aftershave. Aftershave and blood.

And the anger in his eyes. The way he stared at her. He looked more *present* than some of the other infected she'd seen, somehow.

There was a cognisance to his gaze. Like he was fully *there*. There, and angry at her. *Raging* at her.

And then he opened his mouth and he moved his teeth towards her arm.

She watched him. Watched him move in. Again, in slow motion. She heard Dad's shouts. She heard Rufus's barks. But in her mind's eye... in her mind's eye, it was the way he looked at her that she thought of, and that she couldn't *stop* thinking of, above anything. The way he'd looked at her and the way he'd apologised her and told her he loved her, and the way he'd told her to run.

She looked back at him. She looked into his eyes and she expected to see him standing there. She expected to see him like she'd seen him when she was trapped under the crashed car that day. Frozen. Completely frozen.

But...

Dad ran towards her.

He flew into the infected beside her. Rugby tackled him to the ground. Punched him. Then punched him again. Then grabbed a fire extinguisher, swung it at the next of the infected, hurtling towards him.

He looked at her. Looked into her eyes again. "Go," he said. "Now."

She stood there. Frozen. And she understood now. She understood that frozen state. She understood how it was. She understood *why* it was.

She shook her head. "Dad—"

"Go!" he shouted.

She didn't want to go. She didn't want to climb out of that window. She didn't want to leave him. She didn't want to run away.

But as Keira stood there, watching more of the infected run towards Dad, she realised she didn't have a choice.

Nisha needed her.

Her journey wasn't over.

She shook her head. Swallowed a lump in her throat, as tears rolled down her cheeks, and as adrenaline surged through her body.

And then she turned around and she leapt out through the broken window.

She turned around. She looked at Dad. Saw him standing there. Staring at her. Infected hurtling towards him. Screaming.

A smile stretched across his face. A half-smile. Tears staining his cheeks.

"Go," he said. "It's going to be okay, little girl. I promise you everything's going to be okay. I love you, Keira. Go."

She went to open her mouth. To tell him she forgave him. To tell him she loved him. To tell him she understood, and she was sorry for distancing herself from him for so many years, sorry for not giving him another chance to prove to her how much he really cared, sorry for burying her head in the sand instead of confronting her problems, just like she always did.

She wanted to tell him about Blackpool. She wanted to tell him about home. She wanted to tell him about how she'd been living. She wanted to hold him, and she wanted to cry.

She wanted to say so many things to him. So many things, unspoken.

But before she could say a word, two of the infected grabbed Dad, and dragged him away into the darkness.

DAVID

* * *

David watched Keira step away from the window, Rufus by her side.

He went to open his mouth. He went to tell her he loved her. He went to tell her he was so proud of her. Of the woman she'd grown into. The strong woman she'd grown into.

He went to tell her Mum would be so proud of her, too. That she was the apple of her eye.

He went to tell her that he'd always, always understand why she had to distance herself from him, after everything that happened in her childhood. And that he'd always, always be here for her, regardless.

And then he felt the mass of hands grab his body and drag him back into the screaming, infected crowd.

He closed his eyes.

He waited for the pain.

And in his mind's eye, he saw Keira, standing by her mother's side.

He took a deep breath.

He smiled, as tears trickled down his cheeks.
And then the infected surrounded him.

* * *

END OF BOOK 2

Surviving the Outbreak, the third book in The Infected
Chronicles series, is now available.

If you want to be notified when Ryan Casey's next novel is
released—and receive an exclusive post apocalyptic novel totally
free—sign up for the author newsletter: ryancaseybooks.com/
fanclub

Made in United States
North Haven, CT
07 August 2023

40026151R00139